Henry

FORBIDDEN BOOK 2

KATHI S. BARTON

This is a work of fiction. Names, characters, places, and incidents are products of the author's imagination or are used fictitiously and are not to be construed as real. Any resemblance to actual events, locations, organizations, or persons, living or dead, is entirely coincidental.

World Castle Publishing, LLC
Pensacola, Florida
Copyright © Kathi S. Barton 2018
Paperback ISBN: 9798891263604
eBook ISBN: 9781629898841
First Edition World Castle Publishing, LLC, February 5, 2018.
http://www.worldcastlepublishing.com
Licensing Notes
Cover: Karen Fuller
Editor: Maxine Bringenberg

Table of Contents

Chapter 1

Scott sat at the bar and watched the other men and women. He didn't care for beer, not the kind that was served here, but he ordered it so that they'd not run him off. Not that they could, for the most part, but people — humans — had a way of making life difficult when they wanted. It mattered little to them who or what they were up against.

Waiting for the man to come in that was to meet him here, Fred, Scott thought of his life so far. He had not a pot to piss in; not even a pot of any kind, really. And that was the way he liked it. He had money, a great deal of it, but no house, no car, not even a real paying job. He liked his life like it was, without attachments or any kind of strings. It was why he moved from one place to the other without having any roots.

The door opened behind him and he knew that it was Fred. He had an odor about him that even humans could smell. Scott thought him positively repugnant...not just his smell, but everything about him. Even his teeth were a shade of green that made him want to ask if he'd been eating a field.

"I have a handle on her." Scott asked him what sort of handle he had. "The mother is in the hospital now. And when she has the brat, the nurse is going to call me and let me come in. Things are working out much better than you thought they would."

"Doubtful. It's been my experience, and I have a great deal more than you ever will, that once things start to look good, you should look over your shoulder for the next bad vibe. What hospital is she in?"

"Mercy. She's been brought in to be induced, or some shit like that. Something about the kid being a little larger than they thought for her size. That made no sense to me whatsoever. Women get fat when they're having a kid, even I know that." Scott told Fred what they meant. "Oh. Well, why don't they just say she's having a fat kid and that she's too little to do it on her own? You know what that means, don't you? The dick that planted him there was a little one."

And again, Fred's logic wasn't anything that he understood. The man was a wonder, saying things that were so off the wall that Scott wondered if he even knew what they meant. But Scott started thinking about the hospital instead.

"Mercy Hospital is the one that takes in degenerates, correct? I know that place. At one time, the land that it sits on was farmland that belonged to a man who raised cows."

"There ain't no cows there now." Scott said nothing as he took a sip of his now warm beer. "There are a lot of cops hanging around though. I didn't think about all the crime in that place when I was there. Sure can get a man hurt looking for information."

"You've been paid enough." He thought about the baby he was about to take, and what he was to do with it once he had it. Scott had no qualms at all about killing people, but a baby was something way different. He wasn't to drink from it either. Just kill it and be done with it. "Wonder what they want this kid out of the way for. You heard anything?"

"Nope. Just snatch it and bring it to you. I'm guessing you have your orders too." Scott nodded. "I thought so. You've always been close mouthed, ain't you?"

Fred Hogan was anything but close mouthed. Scott would bet money on the fact, too, that the nurse helping him take the little boy knew all about why he needed it done. And most of that would be lies. Fred knew less than he did, and Scott knew very little at all.

The people that wanted the kid taken and killed had only told him that it was a half breed. Nothing more...not even a half breed of what two creatures. They wanted it killed because those kinds of creatures out there would make a bad name for them. He hadn't any idea why that would bother anyone...he was a made vampire himself. But he'd do what he was told, when he was told, and reap the rewards that came along with it. Fred was being paid, yes, but Scott was to get him to leave town as soon as he had the child. It would keep him safe and hopefully away from Devon's fury.

"I'm gonna go out and enjoy the night. I'm thinking that when that nurse calls me, I should be close by. That way I can get it and get back to you before anyone is the wiser. Oh yeah, I forgot. Did you know that the momma isn't taking the kid? She's putting it up for some kind of private thing."

Scott knew that as well. That was why he'd been called in instead of just killing the mom when she was out and about. She was going to live simply because she didn't want the kid.

There were all kinds of people around her all the time

now, he'd noticed. It had taken him the better part of a month to figure out where they'd taken her when she'd disappeared. One day, when he'd gone by the apartment where she was living, she was just gone. And not only that, every bit of her place had been devoid of even her scent. And that was what had Scott worried the most. Someone had a lot of pull in this thing, and he was afraid of who that might be.

Scott figured that there were any number of vampires out there that would want a child. And it would matter little to them if it were something else too. Some of them were with humans that weren't their mates, and needed to have their nests filled up. Like having a child in the house would make anyone happy. It had him at one time, but no more. Shuddering at the thought of a little kid around, he thought of the two kids he'd fathered of his own. Both long dead, but that didn't lessen what they'd made him feel like...a man of the world.

Scott had been a good man, or so he thought. He was also a husband and father that had provided well for his family. However, he didn't find out until later that he'd been a failure at that, to his wife. So one night, in a fit of stupidity, he'd gotten himself turned around on the road and ended up at a party. A bloodletting, he'd figured out later, and he was dinner.

They hadn't killed him, mores the pity, but they had changed him into what he was today. He'd gone back to see his wife and children, spying on them all during the night. But for the most part he left them to assume, as did everyone around, that he'd fallen off a cliff and was dead. Though that didn't mean that he left them on their own.

He provided for them as best he could. Giving them what

money he could steal or earn, he'd leave it on the stoop. And sometimes he'd kill a deer or some other big game and leave it as well. They were well fed, his family, and when he heard that his son was sick, he went to the window to see if he could help him. His wife, Margaret, was there waiting on him.

"I knew it was you." He stared at her from the darkness and said nothing. "You've been the one leaving us food and money, haven't you? Do you have yourself a new whore, Scott? Someone to warm your bed? I hope so." He moved out of the darkness and stood before her. "So you're one of them? The night monsters? I should have known you'd not leave us to our own. Why didn't you just die, Scott? You never do what I need you to do, do you? I had hoped that you'd die from their treatment of you. But I guess I can't be that lucky, can I?"

"You wanted me dead?" She told him how she'd told the vampires that they could have whatever came across them, and to not let it get to her. And that he was to be found, no matter what. "You murdered me? You set them upon me?"

"I did. And I'd do it again if I could have." He asked her why she'd do such a thing. "You think I was supposed to live like this? That I wasn't to have two coins to rub together? To have children that I can no more stand than I could you? Nay, Scott. I don't love you. Never did. You were just a means for me to leave my home. And once I was here, I had plans all along to kill you in your sleep." He had staggered back then, his body just too shocked to do much more than let himself fall to the ground. "Come here no more. I will not have you around, and don't be leaving any food either. I'll not take it from you now that I know that it is from you."

"What of our children? You are nearly starved now." She

11

said that she hoped that they'd die first so that she could leave them in their beds and not return. "You cannot mean that, Margaret. They're just children, small boys that had no part in you and me coming together."

"Had I had the coin, Scott, there would have been no children born at all." She looked at him then, and he could see the hatred that he'd never seen before. "Now, go on your way and don't bother us again. I had no use for you then, and not now either. Be gone."

He left her then, but kept a close eye on the house. After several days he went back to see why there was no smoke curling from the fires. No scents of meat searing in the air. But what he'd seen there had left him broken. His wife hadn't waited for the boys to starve, she'd killed them herself.

Scott had taken their small bodies to the yard that night. After wrapping them in a thick blankets that his own mother had made for them, Scott buried them deep in the ground, and even made a marker for them both. His sons were not yet seven and five, and they were dead by their own mother's hand.

It took him nearly a week to find her. He wasn't surprised to find her in bed with another man. What had surprised him was who it was. He knew as surely as he saw them together that he was his sire. And since he already knew that Margaret had set him up to be killed by them, Scott had had no trouble at all in murdering them both. Even the Council, newly formed back then, had justified his killing of the man who had changed him, without permission.

After that, Scott had wandered around for a long time... several decades as a matter of fact. He had very little use for coin, but would hire himself out as a mercenary when he was approached. It had made him good money, enough that he could do what he wanted, and he had a hell of a reputation. Anyone and everyone that wanted something done that they were squeamish about, he was the man to call.

But even that had grown to be boring. He didn't want to join a nest—he hated people too much—and vampires for the most part were a whiney group of beings. They had to show off their abilities and dress like they had not a care in the world what people thought of them. When in reality they were the vainest people ever made.

He looked to his left when the door opened again. Quincey was the only vampire that he knew that was more well-known than him. When Quincey stared at him, looking at Scott like he knew he was up to something and what it was, Scott felt his balls tighten up and his blood run cold.

"You should go home and forget this." He said he was a man of his word. "Sure you are, Scott. But with this, you'd be better off just going back to your lair and leaving it alone."

"What business is it of yours?" Quincey said nothing but moved down the bar. "I asked you a question—"

He was at Scott's throat before he could even finish the statement, holding him up from the floor without the use of his hands. Scott looked around. He'd get no help from any of the patrons of this place. They were not seeing what was going on. When he was set back down on his feet, Scott sat back on the bar stool and waited.

"Do not presume that you might ask me questions, or that you might demand anything of me, Scott Huff. I will not just end your miserable life, but I will make you suffer in ways that even you, with all your deeds, cannot fathom." Scott believed him. Not only that, but he knew that he'd not

13

just make him suffer, but would do so over a long period of time. "Leave the child where it is. Nothing good will come to you should you take it."

"What makes this child so special is that I was paid a large sum of money to snatch it, then kill it." Quincey nodded, and Scott felt the compulsion ride over his skin when asked who he worked for. "I don't know his name or that of the firm that paid me. It's a front."

"Good to know." Quincey walked away again, and Scott wanted to run. Not just that, but to meet the sun because he was that afraid. "Leave here. Don't return, Scott, or so help me, it'll be the last thing you ever do."

Scott left the bar. He didn't know where to go, but there wasn't any way that he could pass this up. It wasn't just the money he was going to receive, but the man who had him doing it, he had a marker of Scott's. That made it impossible to refuse.

Several hundred years ago, Scott had thought himself so powerful that he'd given tokens to those that helped him. Coins really, that had been marked with his sword. All a person had to do to use it was to give it to him. And then, whatever he was asked to do, he'd have no choice but to do it. The magic, the powerful magic that he'd had put on the coins, was as strong as any that he'd ever used since then, or even before. He'd been a fool to do such a thing, he knew that now.

When Fred found him, just beyond the bar, he looked pale. It wasn't until he was right atop him that Scott could smell the blood. Fred didn't just fall, but fell on him. As soon as he saw the knife in his belly, a scalpel, Scott knew that this was much larger than he'd been told.

"She's had the brat." He asked him where it was. "Don't

know. Two men, they come in and took it. They were ready too. Had all the stuff to take it away."

"What does that mean?" Fred coughed, and blood poured from his mouth. "Fred, who did this to you? Who killed you?"

"I don't know…a man that was sent by someone. He said to tell you his name, but I plum forgot it. You should run." Another cough and more blood, this time thick and dark. "He said to tell you that he's watching you. Am I really dying?"

"You're as good as dead. When did you see him? Fred, when did you see this man?" Scott wished he'd made Fred stay in the bar with him. He'd be alive had he thought of that.

Fred didn't answer him. There was nothing more he could do for the man, so he left him where he laid. Scott pulled shadows around him tightly and walked quickly to his lair. He was going to get answers, and he was going to get them fast. This shit was going to get someone killed, and he thought it might be him.

~~~

Jake sat in the back seat with the baby in the car seat while Forrest drove them home. He'd taken the back roads instead of the highway, and Jake had to laugh at the slow speed he was going. He asked him if he thought they'd get home before she was old enough to vote.

"You drive then, so I can be back there with her. Christ, she's beautiful, don't you think?" He did, and touched his finger gently to her fine cheek. "Her mom, we'll have to tell her about her, don't you think? I mean, the baby's father was your dad, so I'm not sure what you'd say about that. But we're going to make sure that she's well loved, right?"

"Yes. I wasn't sure what to do when they said that her mom died on the table. Do you suppose Stacy just gave up?

15

The last time we spoke to her, she seemed really down." Jake looked at his baby sister. "Forrest, we'll have to keep her safe too. You heard what Quincey told us."

"Yes, I did. And even if he'd not told us about others trying to find her, we'd still care for her." Jake nodded and looked where they were at being home. "We're almost there. To be honest with you, Jake, I was afraid to go straight home. After that man was stabbed in the hallway right outside the delivery room, I just didn't think the straightest route was the best."

"I agree. While I have no idea what that was about, I don't want to take any more chances with her than you do." He wanted to take her out of the seat and hold her in his arms. Just to be assured that she was really theirs.

They had found Stacy about three months ago. She'd been living in a shelter then, her parents having thrown her out when they found out that she was going to have a baby. The poor little thing was younger than him and scared out of her mind that the baby's father would come after her.

It had taken them several trips to see her before she confessed who the father was, and what he'd done to her. As she sat there, sobbing out the story, Jake had held her hand and told her how sorry he was, and then he told her who he was. That nearly got him and Forrest, arrested. It wasn't until he'd had his attorney talk to her that she began to see that he was nothing like the bastard that had raped her, repeatedly, over a two-day period.

They had set her up in a nice apartment, furnished with all the things that she wanted. Stacy wasn't greedy, nor did she want much in the way of money. Just enough to keep her fed and healthy. Her plans for after the baby was born were something they could never get her to share with them. Now, Jake thought he knew why.

"Do you suppose we should name her after her mom?" Forrest just looked at him in the mirror in the car. "I mean, it would be nice, don't you think?"

"I don't know. There were people there looking for her. Calling the baby Stacy might give them a clue as to who she is." That was very true. "I think we should name her Jenna Beck Winslow, just like we decided."

"I miss her; my grandma was the best there was. She'd be over the moon with her, don't you think?" Forrest nodded, both of them still raw about his grandma being killed a few months ago. "My dad goes up for trial soon. You think that is what got her spooked?"

"No, that's not it. Can we talk about it when we get home? I want to tell you what I know. And to be face to face when we do it." He asked if it was bad. "Yes, some of it. But we'll get through it. I've called a couple of buddies of mine to come help us. They're going to be here soon enough."

"I hope they know more about babies then we do. I know we took those classes, but I think this is going to be much harder than we thought." Forrest laughed and said he knew it was going to be. "At least we have those books. Not that I think they're much help either. But we have them."

"Mary said she'd help us too. I know she has a lot of experience with babies." The woman had seven children, ten grandchildren, and two great-grandchildren. If anyone had the knowledge, it would be her. "And I'm really glad that you went shopping yesterday for diapers and such. We'll be set for a while. Doubtful anyone would come snooping around thinking the two of us had a kid."

It had been in the papers that he and Forrest had opened a practice together. And in the same article, it mentioned not only that Jake's ex-wife had been a murderer, having killed her own mother, but that he was gay. Nothing much had been said about it, and because of it, they had a lot more work than they could handle at times. The gay community was supporting them in a big way.

Mary, their housekeeper, met them at the door. She was so excited for them too, and when they'd moved into his grandma's house just after the funeral, she had asked to come with them. The other staff, much older than he had realized, all retired except for Thomas, Grandma's butler and good friend.

After getting Jenna settled in her crib, the two of them fussed in the nursery. Jake knew what they were doing... waiting for her to wake up and need them. And they wanted to be the first to help her. But Mary came in, shooed them out, and told them to find something to do. He and Forrest went to the living room but took the monitor with them. They would not let her down.

"Okay, what I know. Or heard. Quincey is keeping an eye out on things for us. And the reason might surprise you. I know it did me. You have a younger half-brother." Jake leaned back on the couch and asked how old he was. "Just a few years younger than you. He's been notified of your father's arrest, and that your grandma left it all to you. He wants his share."

"And Jenna? What does she have to do with this?" He didn't answer him when Thomas brought them in some scones and tea. Jake wasn't ready to enjoy them just yet. When what was happening and why occurred to him, he didn't even wait for Thomas to leave but blurted it out. "He wants her murdered, then he'll come after me. For the money."

"Yes, that's it." Forrest played with his cup but didn't drink either. "I guess your father's name isn't on the birth certificate. But this guy has had tests done to prove who he is to him. Your father was a real fucker, just in the event you didn't know that. Anyway, your grandma found out about this bastard son before she was murdered. And it wasn't until this morning that I was told about it."

Jake wasn't sure what to say. Or even to do. Protecting his sister was going to be something that he'd devote his life to, but to have his own flesh and blood out to murder them both, her only an infant not even a day old, was almost too much. It made him think that the man was more like his father than he ever wanted to be.

"Do you have anything on him? His name?" Right then, the monitor went off and they both stood up. "You go. I need to digest this information. If you bring her down, that'll be good too. Just...I don't know what to think at the moment."

"All right. But here is what I have on him. And it's not pretty." Forrest started out of the room and stopped. "We'll be all right, Jake. I have friends coming to help us out with this mess."

Jake certainly hoped so. Right now all he could think about was how his life had been full of murderers and murderesses, and he'd been the only sane one in the bunch. Besides his grandma and Forrest, of course.

"Oh, Grandma, I miss you more and more every day. What am I going to do now? What are we going to do now?"

Chapter 2

Henry didn't want to leave his home. Not today. More than likely never. He was in mourning, and it was tearing him apart to be out in the public right now. His mom had passed away last week, and it hurt him more than he could have ever thought it would.

She'd been the only person in the world who had been right by his side when things went to shit. Telling him that it mattered little to her what he was, who he loved, so long as he was happy. There had been few lovers in his life, but not a one of them had ever passed her test. They didn't love him well enough, they were too greedy, or, and this one made him smile, they were much prettier than he was and that wouldn't do. He looked at the headline on the latest newspaper.

"At least they've given me a rest." Henry had been on top of the world in his acting career. He'd never made any kind of secret of his love life. Not even when he'd been as famous as all the other big names. But someone had claimed that he'd taken them to bed against their will, and that was all it took.

Even though it had been proven, over and over, that the man was a liar and that he had faked the pictures that he said he had of them together, Henry was finished as an actor. If he was honest with himself, he thought that perhaps he might have been before this hit. Bored.

Boredom was nothing that he would have claimed before all this. He was sick of having roles that portrayed him as a lover of women. A semi-swashbuckling sort of hero. He knew it was his good looks that had done that. But women were worse than most gay men he knew. Not all, but a few of them. Gossipy, vain, and wanting more than he had to give them. Which was sex.

He looked at the instructions he'd been given to meet with his buddy and longtime friend, Forrest. Forrest was the man that had helped him over the biggest hurdles when it came to being gay. Henry hadn't come out, so to speak, until he met up with the other man. But after he did, becoming happier than he'd been previously, they'd kept in touch…less and less lately, but they had reached out when they could. Then the call had come in about needing his help.

Before becoming an actor, Henry had been a good detective. Not a great one, not without his bit of something extra, but he'd been able to solve more cases than not. He supposed that was why he'd played some kind of gun toting person in his movies. The one that always rescued the damsel and killed the bad guy. He knew just how to hold the gun and fire it without looking like an idiot who had no idea what they were doing.

But he didn't want to go to see his friends right now. He would, he thought—Forrest and Jake were his buddies, probably the only ones he had right now—but he would go and help them. Laughing, Henry thought he was sounding just like the other gays he was making fun of all the time with his mom.

Packing what he needed, Henry was glad now that he'd bought his home and paid cash for it. He didn't have a flashy home...just a two-bedroom ranch that he and his mom enjoyed. They had an ocean view, if they stood up on the house with a ladder and a long telescope...but they could see it. He had a place now that he could fall back on. As well as the money that he'd invested wisely, knowing that his looks wouldn't be something that he could cash in on forever. He just hadn't realized it would be over already.

The trip to the airport was quick. He could fuck with people's mind into not seeing him; a gift from someone he'd helped a few years ago. It was exhausting, this bit of whatever it was, so as soon as his flight was called and he boarded, Henry pulled his hat down over his eyes and slept. Things would be better in the morning, his mom used to say.

The trip was over before he woke up. The gentle touch to his arm made him think of his mom, and he smiled up at the woman. She smiled back and handed him her phone number as she told him that the plane had landed. Tucking it in his pocket, he grabbed his overnighter and left the plane. As he walked by the trash can in the small lobby, he dropped the paper in it. He didn't have time for entanglements anymore.

Forrest was there waiting for him. He was with a good-looking man and was holding a car seat. Henry started laughing even before he got to them. He knew Jake from long ago but was surprised to find him being a mate to Forrest. A great surprise, he thought.

"Henry, you remember Jake Winslow, don't you? Jake

and I have another surprise for you as well." He lifted the car seat up and pulled the blanket off the baby, and just like that, Henry fell in love. "This is our daughter, Jenna. She and Jake are half sister and brother."

"Wow, what a beautiful little girl. And you named her after Jenna. Man, that woman could peel skin off a lemon and never make a face. But I loved her very much. I was so sorry to hear about her passing." Jake thanked him, as did Forrest. "You guys are doing all right then? I mean, it looks like you are."

"We are, really. We've been settling in to be a couple and all that goes with it. But now we have an issue I was hoping you could help me with." Henry nodded and looked around. No one seemed to have any idea who he was, and he liked it. "But, we also want to visit with you, and hope that we can convince you to sell out what you left behind and come stay with us. We have lots of room for both you and your mom."

"I don't know. I didn't tell you before, but my mom passed last week. She had a massive stroke, and died a few hours afterwards." They both hugged him, telling him how sorry they were to hear that. And Henry knew that from these two it was sincere.

"You should just stay with us then." Jake took the carrier from Forrest and they headed for the car. Henry had no luggage but the carry on, so it was a simple matter of just leaving. As soon as he was outside, he knew why he loved this part of the world. The air was much cleaner.

The drive was punctuated with laughter and a little sorrow. He told them of his mom's last moments, and they told him the joys of being parents. He couldn't wait to see them in action, the two of them just learning how to change diapers and get up in the middle of the night. Christ, he had really missed this...friendship. True friendship.

"We're working on selling Jake's house. I sold mine a few weeks ago, and we're just taking our time with the second one. It's huge as well. But too many sour memories for us right now. We might rent it if we can't sell it, but we're open to anything right now." Forrest fed the baby her bottle while Jake drove. "Also, Thomas is staying with us, as is our housekeeper, Mary. She's a blast and has been a tremendous help with Jenna."

When they pulled up in front of the home of Jenna Winslow, he stood there just letting the memories roll over him. He'd only known the woman for a short time, in the last year or so, but he had fallen in love with her. She was crass when necessary, and she always told it like it was. Henry thought he could have been a very happy man, just listening to her tell stories of her life.

Henry got to feed little Jenna while he told them what had happened to his career. He skipped over the ugly parts, saying only that he'd been dropped by his agent at the very first sign of trouble, and Henry had been all right with that.

"Mom told me from the first it would be a scandal, and that I might as well be as up front about it as I could. And I was. But this thing, it was as if no one had ever heard the facts before, and decided that I was some sort of monster by just being who I was." Jake said that he'd seen one of his movies, when Forrest said that he knew him. "Yeah, I bet that was fun. I haven't seen them, not really. I'd go to the premier, but I didn't keep up with the movie. Mom would tell me later who was there and how they were reacting to certain parts. But for the most part, we people watched."

After they had a wonderful dinner, they sat at the table and talked some more. It was wonderful to just be himself. Talk to friends about his feelings and know that they'd never make him feel badly for them. Nor would they say anything to anyone else. He had missed this part of his life most of all.

"Forrest tells me that you have a freaky ability. He didn't tell me what it was, but he said that you would. I have to tell you, I'm intrigued by it. Forrest also said that you were a detective at one time."

Henry laughed and said he didn't know if it was freaky or not, and yes, he'd been a detective. "I guess they sort of went hand in hand. I can see ghosts." Jake started to laugh, and then realized that he was serious. "When I was just a kid, six or so, I was in a horrific accident with my father. He died—seatbelts weren't that big a deal then—and I was in trauma for about six weeks. My mom wasn't with us or she might have died too. A logging truck overturned atop us."

"Oh my goodness. How on earth did you survive that?" Henry told him that he'd been asleep on the floorboard in the backseat. "Wow, how lucky were you? I mean, not completely lucky...you did lose your father, but.... I'm going to shut up now."

"I saw my dad's ghost the first thing when I woke up. He told me that I had to not say anything to anyone, or he'd be in trouble for visiting me. Being a kid, I thought that he was in after hours or something. Anyway, when Mom showed up, she told me how Dad had died, and I told her that he was with us, in the room. As you can imagine, that didn't go over well either. Mom believed me, but the doctors and nurses, they thought that I had some sort of trauma to my head. More than they had thought. Mom and I talked it over, and I was only to talk to him and about him when we were alone. My childhood after that was a series of ghosts popping in and out, having me do things for them."

"What sort of things, if you don't mind me asking?" Henry looked around the room and back at them. "Someone is here, isn't there? My grandma?"

Henry knew he was breaking the rules by telling Jake, but decided that this time it was worth it. "Yes. She's fading, which means she isn't here to need much. Jenna wants you to know that she loves you both, very much." Jake asked him where she was, and he pointed to her. "She said that she knows that the man coming for you, Devon Winslow, is going to cause you trouble, and she wishes that she had told you sooner."

"Grandma, we miss you so much. Did you see your namesake? Little Jenna is going to know all about you." Henry watched her travel to the newborn and lean down to look at her. Jake said nothing more as Forrest held him while he cried. "I wish she had let him shoot me."

"She said for you to buck up and shut up. How would you have been able to save this little one had you been dead?" Henry laughed when she cursed. "She has a streak in her, doesn't she? But she wants you to do something for her; she asks that you not dwell too much on the fact that she died, but be happy for the time that the three of you had together."

"I'll try." Jenna told him he'd better do more than try, and Henry relayed that message too. "All right. I can do that, but I'm not saying I won't slip up, but I'll do it."

Jenna looked at Henry, her eyes filled with love, and told him that she was glad that he was there for them. As he nodded at her, she told him the rest of what she needed to have them know. Then she told Henry to come and live here with them for a time, but to make plans to stay forever. He needed them as much as they did him. Henry looked at the two men that in a short amount of time he had become closer with than before.

"There is a man that she wishes for you to contact. The name is written on her stationery in her desk in her room. In the smaller drawers. He has some information on Devon that you might be able to use. Also, she said for you to clean out her things and move on. This house was never meant to be a tomb for her."

"We've been doing that a little at a time." Forrest said that it was more difficult than they thought it would be. "Tell her that we'll have a large yard sale and have it all on the front lawn. She can tell us if we have it for too much or too little."

Henry watched her laugh, and when she touched the baby once more, she blew them all three a kiss and then looked at him again.

"Sell it all and come here. I've spoken to your mother—what a wonderful person she is—and she said that she'd be so happy if you came to be with people you love instead of all that out there. And when you come here, to buy Jake's house and live in it. You could also take my son's home, but that would be messy. Trina had a terrible sense of style, though not as bad as Carol did, but pretty bad."

Henry told them that she was leaving, and she may or may not be back. Then when she was gone, he handed little Jenna to Forrest and went out to the deck. He needed a moment, and knew that they'd understand. Living here, it would be good, but he didn't know if he'd be welcome.

~~~

28

Paddy wasn't sure what he was supposed to do with the message he'd received. But he wasn't in any place he could make a call to figure it out. He didn't know a Winslow, nor did the name Stout ring a bell. But that wasn't the strangest part. Two weeks ago he'd had an attorney approach him from the firm Stout and Winslow, but nothing had ever materialized with it.

Right now, however, wasn't the time to be making calls. He was on a job. Paddy looked through his binoculars once more at the three men across the street. Today was going to be the day; at least he hoped to Christ it was.

Five months prior he'd been tipped about a huge deal going down. What sort of deal, he had no idea. There were all sorts of things that came to mind in a city this big, but no one seemed to have clues as to what it was. He couldn't even get his boss to get in on it.

"Just do your job, Garrett. There's nothing going on. Just go out, arrest the bad guys, and go home at night." He laughed when he did. "You're a good detective, and it might get you killed one day."

The more he thought about that, the more he thought it had been a threat. Not that he mistrusted his boss…Captain Walton hadn't ever given him any indication that he was anything but a lazy cop. Like most of the men he worked with. But today it had been kind of odd when Paddy was told to come have a look-see about a deal he'd heard about.

"That deal going down. I heard something that might interest you about it." Paddy nodded, leery right away. "There is a meeting of sorts in front of the Gambler Building. Do you know where that is?"

"Yeah, down on Fifth. About the worst part of town."

Walton said that was it. "Do you have any idea who the players might be? What is going down? Anything more?"

"No, I don't." The captain looked around, his voice going very low, like he was afraid that someone else might have heard him speaking. "You go there and see what's going on. Don't engage, Garrett. Do you hear me? For Christ's sake, don't engage."

And now here he was, sitting atop the building not across from the Gambler building, but one to the left of it. Paddy still had no idea what it was he was looking for. It was, as far as he could see, just three men, talking and waving their arms a lot.

When he looked to his right, he saw three men in uniform walking around the building across from him. Paddy was just about to rise up, to wave at them to tell them where he was, when he noticed they were hot. Their guns were not only out, but their fingers were at the ready. Staying where he was, his body nearly flat with the roof, he pulled his gun out as well. Something was about to hit the fan, and he was thinking it was going to be him.

The men were walking around like they didn't care who saw them. Paddy wished that he could see the three men at ground level, to see if they were a part of this shit. But to raise his head meant he'd lose it, and he sort of enjoyed having it right where it was. Watching the men, however, he got the feeling that they were all in on this together, and he realized that his boss had warned him as best he could.

When one of them tore his face mask off, Paddy was stunned to see who it was…his partner for the last three weeks, Grant Dudley. He waved at the men below, he assumed, and told them that Paddy must not have shown up. While he was talking to the three men, the other two cops joined him and shot at the men below. By the return fire, and it suddenly being cut off, he assumed that they were all dead. Christ, this was a nightmare.

Just as they were turning to leave, Paddy's fucking cell phone went off. He was sure that he'd muted it, but it mattered little now. The three cops turned in his direction and opened fire.

Little time to aim and fire back, he pointed in the general direction as to where they were and fired. Moving backwards, crawling on his belly, Paddy knew he was as good as dead. When they had to reload, thankfully, he jumped up, fired at them this time, and ran. The first bullet took him to the ground, but he was up and going again before he was able to assess the damage.

Running for his life took on a whole new meaning to him as he darted by the men that had been talking. One of them was the butcher from across the road from where he lived; the guy who ran the shelter was one of the other men. But the third, he had no idea. Paddy was just glad that he'd been on the wrong building when this started.

Paddy wasn't super smart, but he wasn't stupid either. He'd taken the warning that he'd gotten from Walton to heart, stashing him a car, money, and clothing, then, at the last-minute, throwing in several first aid kits. He made his way there now. He was getting weaker—he could hardly run as fast as he thought he needed to—but when he slipped into a building that he knew as well as his own apartment, Paddy finally had time to look at himself.

He had one gunshot wound to his upper thigh…an inch or so more and he'd be a eunuch. The second bullet had gotten him in the chest plate. While it didn't penetrate, it still hurt like a mother fucker. The third one was in his right side, just below the vest he'd worn, and it was a through and through.

But just because the bullet had gone all the way through him, it didn't mean he was out of danger. Pulling out his phone to see who the fucker was he was going to have to murder now, he didn't recognize the number. With bloodied fingers he hit call back, and was surprised when it was answered right away.

"Who the fuck is this, and why the fuck are you calling me? Do you fucking know that you almost got me killed? Mother fuck. As it is now, I might fucking bleed to death before I can find someplace safe to lay low." He looked down at his body and wanted to just lay down and try to repair himself. "What the fuck do you want?"

"Where are you?" The second man's voice was harder, like he was in charge of a large corporation. "Tell me your location and we'll come for you. It'll be safe, I promise."

"I should have known better than to do this. He tried to warn me." Paddy was getting weaker by the minute. He didn't think he'd die—he'd not be that lucky—but he didn't want to be laying there in the cold building either. He told the person on the other end where he was going to be, if he could get up and get going. "Right now I'm sitting in a parking garage about ten feet inside the entrance. You'll be able to find me; I'm the dead guy in the puddle of his own blood."

"We're leaving now. Just don't die." Paddy said he'd give it his best shot. "Good. We'll be there. Just hang on. I don't know how long it will take us to get to Cincinnati, but we're leaving right now."

When the line went dead, Paddy laughed. He didn't even get a name. For all he knew it could have been someone that was with the guys who had killed those people. When his phone rang a second time he didn't bother answering it. It was too much work, and he was suddenly exhausted. The sound of his incoming message ringing had him picking it up, and then laughing again.

My name is Forrest Stout. I'll be with two men and a baby. The movie came to mind, the one with nearly the same title. *Don't give up. We'll be there soon.*

Paddy closed his eyes. He didn't have the first clue why he believed the man who he'd spoken to briefly. But he did. There was also something calming about him. His take charge attitude should have pissed him off, but it hadn't.

When he heard a noise, he looked up to see his partner; Double D he'd been calling him, for Dudley Do Right. He knew now that the name was so far off the mark that he was going to start calling him Dudley Dumbass. Paddy didn't make a sound as he moved through the closed gates and within about five feet of where he was.

"Dudley, he there?" With a quick look around he turned to the man outside and shook his head. "Come on then. We have to make sure he's dead. Elsewise we can't get him for murder without him coming back to bite us in the ass. He was wearing his body cam."

Paddy looked down at the camera on his chest and realized that he was wearing it. Christ, he wondered how much, if anything, he had been able to capture. Surely he would have been able to at least catch them firing at him.

When Dudley left the garage, Paddy tried to move back more in the shadows. It was too hard; his body was just too heavy and it hurt to move much more than a couple of inches. Looking at his phone, turning the sound off, he closed his eyes again. Whatever came, he supposed, was going to come. There wasn't much he could do about it.

"Officer Garrett?" He opened his eyes and tried to make out the person who'd spoken. "My name is Forrest. We spoke on the phone. We're here."

"I don't know you. Why are you here?" If he answered him, Paddy didn't hear it. The two men standing there looked large enough to lift a house. "Where is the baby? You said that you had a baby."

"She's in the car with my mate." Well, that sounded like a good place to be. "Come on now, we're going to lift you up and put you in the back of the van. I have some medical supplies back there to fix you up."

"I have money." He said that he did too. "No, I mean, I have a car stashed with clothing and cash. I'll need it. My guns are in it too."

"I'll drive it. Where are the keys?" The man lifted him up in his arms like a small child after he told him the model, make, and year of his car, as well as where the keys were hidden. "You're bleeding pretty badly. Why didn't you shift?"

"The bullets are still there. And I've lost too much blood." He tried to see the man's, Forrest's, face, but it was too hard to make him out. "How did you know?"

"I'm a tiger. Forrest Stout." He nodded and felt himself being laid on a soft mattress. "I have blankets too. And while Jake drives us home, I'm going to work on you. All right?"

"You got anything to knock me out? It'll take a lot." Forrest said that he didn't, but he knew where he could get something. After that, Paddy just let things take him under.

Paddy drifted in and out of consciousness. He would wake in pain so bad that he screamed out with it, and once he was pretty sure that a baby crying woke him. All the time, there was Forrest telling him that he was safe and that he would make sure he lived. Paddy wasn't sure why, again, that he believed him, but he did. And that should have scared him enough to stay away. But he let the pain take him under once again.

Chapter 3

Devon asked him to repeat himself. There wasn't any way that he'd just told him that he was finished. He had his marker, for fucks sake. He'd better do what he wanted him to do.

"I said that there is too much heat on this right now. And I don't have any idea who the people were that took the kid since someone killed my partner, right there in the hospital." Devon wanted to tell him he'd done it and blamed it on someone else, but he didn't. Scott continued speaking to him like he was an idiot, and he had to slow his speech down so that he'd understand. "The mother died just after giving birth so with that, I can't track the kid. Also, come to find out, it's not a boy, as we'd been told, but a girl. Some guy and his spouse took her as soon as she was released."

"How is that even possible? I thought there had to be some tests done or something. Like maybe, I don't know, blood work or some shit." Scott only sat there, staring at him like he wasn't paying attention to how powerful he was. "You said you're going to quit this job. Do you have any idea what I can do to that so-called reputation you have right now? I can and will ruin you."

Scott stood up. He was a giant of a man. Not fat; Devon doubted that fat would dare touch him. But he was tall, at least seven feet, though it could have been that Devon was only five feet five. It was why he sat whenever he had to talk to someone. He didn't want them knowing of his small stature.

"Are you trying to impress me, Scott? It won't work. I have men like you killed daily." He didn't, but Scott didn't have to know that. "Sit down until I tell you other—"

His throat was being squeezed tightly. Even had he wanted to inhale, there wasn't any place for it to come in. As he struggled to get whatever tightness it was from around his throat, Scott walked around his office like nothing was going on.

"I don't like you. And as I'm sure you're aware right now, I can kill you without lifting a finger. When I tell you things are too hot right now, you should take it as gospel." The pressure was let off and he inhaled sharply. But it only lasted long enough for him to breathe once before it was gripping him again. "I'm an old and powerful vampire. And due to the fact that you lied to me, twice now, about things going on, I can only assume that you have no idea who Quincey is."

The pressure was released when Scott snapped his fingers. Sitting in the chair again, Devon glared at the man as he tried to get his breathing under control. Devon was going to kill him. Shoot him in the head and be done with this fucker.

"I can read your mind, Devon. All of it. Even though you think that I can't because I haven't had a bite of you, you'd be wrong about that as well. Do not fuck with me." Devon

38

leaned back in his chair, his heart now pounding in his chest. "I can smell your fear of me. Hear that little cold heart of yours going pitter patter while you think of your options. I will tell you this…you reach for that gun and I'll slice your throat up, and you'll be dead before anyone can save you."

"What makes you so bad assed?" He didn't answer him. Devon didn't want Scott to think he had the upper hand when it was obvious to both of them that he did. "I heard the name Quincey before and figured that you'd not know him. Apparently he's more well-known than you are. What makes him such a big deal? Perhaps I should have hired him instead of you."

The laughter was scary. It wasn't humor filled like he would have expected. It was more like he was angry. And maybe he was, but Devon had hired him to do a job and he was damn well going to do it.

"So, you killed the man that had my coin. That means, in the event you didn't know it, that I owe you nothing." Scott snapped his fingers and the gold coin was in his hand. When he began twirling it around his fingers, over top then under, Devon watched, mesmerized. "The man you took this from, he should be avenged, and I might do that. But not today, though perhaps tomorrow or the next. Then there is the death of my friend, Fred. You murdered him for what reason…to prove a point? It's lost on me now."

"Do you honestly think that I'm supposed to be worried about you? I'm not." Scott told him not to lie. "I'm not lying. You're not worth it for me to make up an untruth just to impress you."

"I'm not impressed by you, Devon. But what you should be worried about is how much information I have on you now. Like this family event that you have going on. And now I know the reason that you wanted that baby to be dead." Scott tsked at him. "To kill a child over money? Not even I, a monster of the night, would think to do such a thing."

"You were going to kill him for me when you didn't know, so don't be so high and mighty now." Scott told him that it was a female, and he'd had no intentions of killing the child, ever. "Sure you didn't. What were you going to do, Scott? Change it into what you are? Perhaps take the thing to your bed?"

Devon knew the moment the words left his mouth that he'd gone too far. Not only was his throat closed off again, but he was lifted to the ceiling of his office and banged against it several times. When he started getting sick, his head splitting from the lack of air and the pain, he passed out.

When he woke, he was alone in the room. The paperwork that he'd had on his desk seemed to still be there. And when he got up from the floor, he had to hold onto anything close by so that he didn't fall over. Dizzy and his head pounding, Devon made his way to his chair.

There was a written note on his desk, but he couldn't make it out. Laying his head on the blotter, he inhaled through his mouth and out his nose several times as he tried to get the black spots he was seeing to disappear. It took him a good fifteen minutes to be able to raise his head up, and another hour before he could read the note.

The handwriting was fancy. Script like none that he'd ever seen. The red ink was darkening now, and he had a moment to wonder where he'd gotten it. The pen alone would have been beautiful, he thought, and as he started to read the note, his skin began to crawl along his body.

40

Hello, Devon. I couldn't find an inkwell, so I had to improvise. If I were you, I'd get the wound that I had to use at your throat cleaned before you get sepsis and die. But I digress. I will no longer be in your employment. I have, however, taken the money you had in your safe. Why do you have one, by the way, if you aren't going to keep it locked? Thank you. And since you have fucked me over, I am going to do the same to you. Happy hunting.

Then it was signed with a single S.

Getting up, still holding on so that he'd not fall, he stood in front of the mirror over his file cabinet. There it was, a large hole in his throat with a wad of tissue stuck in it. Removing the tissue caused it to bleed again, so he held it there. Going to his phone, he called an ambulance, terrified to get in his car and drive to the hospital.

"You're going to pay, you fucking bastard."

While waiting for the ambulance to get there, he made him a list of all the things that he was going to do to Scott when he saw him again. And he was going to find this Quincey person. He was going to do this job for him now. And he'd allow him to kill Scott if he wanted to. This was war, and he was going to win this shootout.

The doctors at the hospital asked him several times what he'd done. At first he'd told them just what had happened. That a vampire had come into his home, accosted him, and then used his blood to write him a letter. But no matter how many times he'd shown the said letter to them, then later the police, no one saw what was written there. Devon ended up just saying that he'd fallen, and he didn't remember.

The bumps on his head had proven that for him. He

41

required fourteen stitches in his head to put it back together, as well as twenty-three in his neck. But the worse part of it was that he couldn't talk. He could, but the doctor advised against it, saying that he had some muscle damage there, and if he wanted it to heal correctly, he shouldn't speak. That might be the most difficult thing he'd ever been made to do, he thought.

After being given a note pad and a pencil, he was sent home. He would have to be on a liquid diet for the next two weeks, the same amount of time he shouldn't speak. That was also to keep the muscle in his neck from being hurt. And he wasn't to strain himself when trying to take a shit. Those, of course, weren't the exact words the doctor had used, but it was the same thing. Devon had never realized how many muscles were attached to his neck.

Just to make sure he wasn't being punked, he sat on the toilet when he got home and knew that he'd been told the truth. He'd nearly screamed when he sat down to take a dump, and it felt like his neck was being torn out. That fucking vampire was going to pay for this.

Devon hadn't thought of his father since he'd been a kid. He'd come around, knock his mom around a bit, and leave some money. It wasn't ever all that much…a few hundred dollars. But Mom would stash it away like she was saving for some big television. It never materialized, but he did have big hopes for the money.

When he was seventeen, he found out that Jacob Winslow was worth a great deal of money. And that he had a family… one that was legal, not like Devon and his mom were; him a bastard, his mom Jacob's whore. The next time he came around, Devon was ready for him. However, he never expected the man to be ready for him as well.

"You're not mine." He said that he was, that his mom had his birth certificate, hoping he'd not want to see it because it was a lie...like a lot of things he had done since then. "Yes, I'm sure she does. And there are a lot of kids out there, younger and older than you, that have my name on them. Doesn't mean shit. I had the perfect boy, and now he's gone. I was left with one that is stupider than you are."

"I'm not stupid." The fist to the side of his head had been quick, and Devon had laid there staring at the man. "What the fuck did you do that for?"

"You think to blackmail me for money? Well, good luck with that. My mom is the one that holds my purse strings, and the sooner she's dead, the better. I might even do it myself." Devon found out recently that he had done it, firing at his other son, the one he had by marriage, and hit his mom instead.

So now, before all the money was gone, he was planning to get as much of it as he could lay his hands on. If he had to kill off some of his siblings to get it, then so be it. Devon wasn't going to be left out in the cold ever again.

Taking one of the pain pills, he went to bed. Devon couldn't believe all the shit that had gone down today, and how much he'd not gotten accomplished. He didn't have the brat killed. Nobody working for him, and the one person that he thought he had in the bag had gone so far off the reservation that he doubted he'd ever get him roped in. Laughing at his ability to use something he'd read today, he thought that he'd gotten pretty good at working them into his daily activity. Having a quote of the day had been paying off.

"Now I have to find my big brother and see what the fuck

I have to do to get him out of the picture." Devon figured that he might be the hardest one to kill off without anyone taking notice. "But I can do it. I'm a Winslow, and I get things done."

~~~

Henry wasn't entirely sure what was going on right at the moment, but he was willing to help out. He had a shitload of things that he could be doing, he supposed, but sitting with the shot-up man was calming for him.

He was older than he'd thought he was. Not ancient, but older than he was by a few years. He'd seen his driver's license when he'd been brought in, and he was a wolf. That part he'd not known until Forrest told him. Since he was resting well, and all the bullets had been removed, once he woke and shifted, he'd be nearly at one hundred percent. The only thing that had worried any of them was that he never let go of his gun.

Patrick—he knew his name now—hadn't fired on them when he was in pain. But he never was awake long enough to do more than scream a great deal and then pass out. Henry thought that his pain threshold was huge. He'd have been whimpering like a baby had it been him. Looking at the spirit that entered the room with them, he asked if things were all right.

Wally, that's all he knew of his name, had been with Henry since he was a kid. The ghost had told him about what he could do now, how to hide his knowledge from others, from the living, and had helped in ways that he was sure were not as legal some might think.

Wally could go through walls, bank vaults, as well as any kind of locked place there was. And while he was going through such things, he could relay back to him what was there, who might be waiting for him, and for what reason. It had saved his ass a great many times over the years.

"I've found the man you wished." Wally looked at the man on the bed. "He is not human, is he?"

"No, he's a wolf. What have you found out about Devon Winslow?" Wally moved around the room, walking, for the most part for Henry's benefit. It sort of creeped him out when Wally flew around the room. "Wally? What did you find out?"

"Devon Winslow isn't a nice man. A vampire has bitten him recently and sent him to the hospital. I believe him to be the one that was sent to murder the child." He moved to the nice shelf of books that was on the other side of the room. "Someday I'd like to learn to read. Do you think it would be hard to teach me?"

"I don't know. But if you'd like, I can work on that." Wally thanked him. "What makes you think this vampire was hired by Devon? And what does he have to do with this man?"

"I am working on that. The spirits at the hospital, they're difficult to speak to. They're so bored that they tell me of everything that killed them. There are some that claim they were killed by the same hand." Wally looked at him. "It took me some time to work out that a hand wasn't going around the place murdering people. I will need that explained to me again, the way sentences work out."

"I'll do that too. Anything else you know?" Wally continued to walk around the room again. Not touching anything…he couldn't do that. And over the decades the two of them had been together, he knew that while he couldn't rush Wally, he did have to keep him focused. "I have spoken to the woman that lived here. She is receptive of you being here with us. But you have to find her when there is trouble, so she can come back and help."

"I have met her. Her name is Jenna, like the child down the hall. She can see me; did you know that? The baby?" Henry told him that he'd heard that, but never knew for sure. "Yes, when I go to speak to her, she quiets down. She is very happy that she is here with everyone."

Henry looked at the bed and saw that Patrick was awake and staring at him. He started to explain to him what he was doing, but the man looked right at Wally and asked if he had died.

"Yes, some time ago. I don't know when, but he said that it wasn't nearly as busy as it is now, and there were no televisions. I have narrowed it down to right around the late eighteen hundreds, due to the way he's dressed and his use of the English language." Patrick looked at him. "I can't believe you can see him."

"Yeah, well, I was asking if I was dead, not the ghost. And I figured since you were having a conversation with him, I'd either died or you were a necromancer." He said he wasn't that, but just a man who had contacts with the other world. "And that's not a necro?"

"No. I don't call them from their graves. And so far as I know, I can't make them go back to wherever they came from. I might be able to, but none of them have bothered me too much, so I didn't think to try." Wally came to stand over the bed where Patrick was. "Can you hear him as well? Or just see him?"

"Both." Patrick put out his hand to touch Wally and it went right through him. It had been the same for him when he'd first seen a ghost. "This is fucking freaky, just so you know."

"You should live with them on a daily basis. You get used to them after a while. I'm Henry Myers. You're Patrick Garrett." He told him to call him Paddy. "All right. Do you remember much about coming here? Why you're here or anything?"

"Yes, I think I was sold upriver and left to die. And if I don't miss my bet, I'm being blamed for the deaths of those men in front of the Gambler Building." Henry told him he was. "Yeah, thought so. And I'm in some man's house by the name of Still...no, Stout. Three men and a baby."

"Yes, that's right. I never thought of it like that, but yes, I drove your car back here. And Jake had a friend of his go over your car to make sure that there weren't any devices on it. It's clean." Paddy nodded. Wally leaned down and pressed his head into the chest of Paddy and Henry stood up. "Wally, you're being rude again."

"His wounds are doing well. I have seen that you have no broken ribs, but you are badly bruised. You will mend in a couple of days, less if you can shift." Paddy thanked him. "No worry for that. It was my pleasure. You should also know that the men who shot at you, they're all dead. You killed one of them when you were attacked, and the second one died later from his wounds. The third was killed by Quincey. He's a good friend of the lady of the house."

Paddy looked at Henry. "Jenna Winslow. She was murdered a few months ago by her son. He's in prison right now." Paddy leaned back on the pillow, then sat up quickly. "Are you in pain? Can I get you something?"

"Winslow? As in Stout and Winslow? Someone from that place contacted me a few weeks back, but they didn't return my call. Then I get this.... What's going on here?" Henry said that he didn't know. But they'd been told to find him, and they did. "I don't know anyone by that name. I'm not even sure why you'd contact me."

"To be honest, I don't know a great deal either. I'm friends with Forrest. He's the one that talked to you before this. And his mate is Jake. He is...was Jenna Winslow's grandson." Henry tried to think what else was going on, but he was distracted by the handsome man on the bed. "Devon Winslow is a half-brother to Jake. Or so he says. He has decided that since he's Winslow's son, the one in prison, he wants his share of the money Jenna left Jake. And his share is amounting to a great deal if he can kill off Jake and little Jenna. Did that even make sense?"

"Yes, you did well. So, where is this Devon person? And how do you know he is the half-brother?" He told him what he knew. "Tests can be fucked with. And what I know of this jerk so far, he would pay dearly for having one faked. I'm assuming that it's a great deal of money. Only because of the way this one room looks."

"Billions. Jake already has that much, more with his grandma's money, which, to be honest, I'm not sure how this kid thinks he's going to get any of it. She specifically left it to Jake. The will even states that no other Winslow, by marriage or not, can inherit any of it. And none was left to Jacob, who is Jake's father." Henry wasn't sure he was doing a good job of explaining any of this. His mind was on other things, like did Paddy taste as good as he looked. "You might be better off talking to Jake and Forrest. They're downstairs. I can go get them."

"Is there something wrong?" Henry asked him what he meant. "Well, you've been like a jackrabbit since I woke up.

Either I hurt you, which I'm profoundly sorry if I did, or there is something else. What is it?"

"I don't know. I mean, I've been in here for the last few hours, just thinking and feeling calmed by you being here. I haven't any idea why." He nodded, but Henry felt the need to explain more. "I've just lost my mom, and I've been out in Hollywood for a few years. It's fast there...cars, people, and things going on all the time. Here, sitting in this room with you, I feel relaxed. But now that you're awake, I feel the need to run."

"I won't hurt you." Henry nodded, thinking that if the man knew what he'd been thinking about doing to him, he most certainly would. "I'm a wolf. Full blooded, and a cop. Not a beat cop anymore, but one that does the nasty stuff. Please sit down."

Henry sat, and Wally came to stand beside him. He said he needed to talk to him. Whatever he had to say, he told him that he could say it in front of the other man. Wally was shaking his head quickly and told him to come now.

Wally walked through the door and Henry told Paddy that he'd be back. Opening the door, he was surprised to see both Jake and Forrest coming down the hall. They told him that Wally had come to get them.

"I have something to tell you. It is important. The man in there, he has a sister that depends on him. She is...I'm not sure of the word. Her mind is not right." Henry asked why that was important. "They are after her. The men that went after your mate, they're after her to get him to come back."

"We have to go get her." They all turned to Paddy when he was standing in the doorway. "I can't let them hurt her. I have to go."

49

"Wait." No one moved when Jake spoke. "I'll send someone for her. I can send Quincey if he can do it."

Almost as if he had been summoned, the vampire was in the room with them. After Paddy gave him the information as to where she was and the safety word to get her, Quincey disappeared.

In seconds he was back, a limp woman in his arms. Henry went to her when Paddy did to see if she had been hurt.

"Nay, I'd never harm such a beauty. She is merely resting. When I went to get her, she was most upset. Not at me, but at an orderly who meant to take advantage of her." Paddy asked who it was. The anger that they heard was not just evident on his face, but his wolf rolled over him as well. "You need not worry. He has been taken care of."

No one questioned the vampire, but Paddy did thank him. When he reached for his sister, Quincey said that he'd take her to one of the bedrooms. He told Paddy that he should shift, there was much to tell them on what he'd been able to find out.

Henry was going down the stairs with the rest of them when it occurred to him what Wally had said. He'd called Paddy his mate. Looking for the ghost to ask him what he'd meant, Jake asked him if he was all right. Nodding, he followed them to the big living room. But he would talk to the man. There wasn't any way that he had that right.

Chapter 4

Scott hadn't any idea how to contact Quincey. He was a powerful vampire, and most that knew him were terrified of him. So was Scott. But he had to talk to him, about a great many things. But first and foremost, he needed to tell him he was sorry.

And he was. Scott had been lied to and conned. He wasn't sure that the man would believe him, but he really needed to make amends. For his part in the baby scheme, his friend getting killed, as well as just being a stupid vampire all these years.

The air around him tightened and he turned to see that he wasn't alone in the room. The library held a special place in his heart, and was a place that he came to often. It amazed him how many books were in such a wonderful place.

"You're looking for me?" Nodding, Scott fell to his knees, then his belly. "I don't know what you think you're doing by submitting to me now, Scott, but I have no use for a man such as you."

"I understand that, Lord Quincey." He hadn't been surprised to find out that the older vampire was a lord, but he had been surprised about his worth. The man was a billionaire several times over. "I wished to tell you that I no longer work for Devon. He lied to me. I guess I should have expected it, coming from a man that would wish a child dead."

"This man, he is a Winslow?" He said he claimed that he was. "I have some dealings with him that I'd like to end. He is a man without any worth, and someone that should be dead."

"I couldn't agree more." Scott looked up, then sat up on his knees when Quincey told him to. "I have some information on him. I was at his home when I found out that the marker he'd given me to have me do the job was stolen. But he isn't a Winslow. The blood test that he had done is a fake. I took what was in his safe that night and sent him to the hospital. But there was nothing in there to indicate that he was a Winslow."

"You have it still?" He said that he did, and laid the fat envelope in front of him. "Why is it that people keep such things close at hand? Things that could incriminate them should anyone wish to look? Humans. It's small wonder that they're forever failing at things."

"Devon, he wants to kill both the child and the man he says is his half-brother. He had an argument with a man named Jacob. Jacob had plans to kill off or at least make the elder Winslow, his mother, pass early. He had been cut off from her funding." Quincey sat down on one of the many chairs and invited him to do so as well. "I should like to help you with this man. He has lied to me, as I said, but he also killed a friend of mine and blamed it squarely on you."

"This I know as well. But as I said, I have no use for help. Whatever you have given me, I will reward you in any way that is not binding nor will harm others." Scott said that he didn't want anything. "I have looked into your life as well. You were changed against your will. I will tell you that you were supposed to die that night, not become a night walker such as I am."

"She told me. My wife." Quincey nodded, and said he'd heard that Scott had killed her and his sire. "I did. She murdered my sons, both little boys that had not done anything to her, only to be my sons. I would, if you would allow it, tag Devon and give you information as you need it."

"There is something that you can do for me. It doesn't involve this case, but another. There is a police officer, his name is Patrick Garrett. Just recently he was to be murdered by some of his own. I would like for you to go there and find out why and who is involved in that." He said that he could do that. Work as a cop with them. "You could do that? Blend in with them?"

"I was a police officer at one time. I could do it. I would enjoy helping. This man...he is a friend of yours too?" Quincey told him what the connection was. "It is amazing to me sometimes that people can be connected in ways that you never realize. Yes, I'll go there today and figure out what I can. But I don't know how to contact you."

"Contact me through Jake and Forrest." Quincey gave him the phone number. "They both know how to reach me. And tell no one, Scott. This could be the death of a great many people, including you."

"I won't. On this I will swear my life." Quincey asked him why he was going to do this, for people he didn't know. "The death of my children changed me. The murdering of my wife and sire changed me once again. I should like to leave this world in a better place than when I was here. I have not been a good man. Not for a very long time."

Quincey seemed to be thinking about his answer. And when he stood up, putting out his hand, Scott was under no delusions that it was in friendship. More that he was getting his scent. Taking the strong hand in his, Scott felt the connection all the way to his heart.

"You fuck with me on this and you will regret it." Scott told him that he understood and would go willingly to his death. "Willingly or not, this is my family that you'd be hurting, and I protect what is mine."

"I understand." He did too. Scott understood the meaning of family more than most, and the loss of them.

He had something to do and it would be good. Scott signed into the computers that were in the library for anyone to use and hacked into the police station. It was much easier than he thought it should have been, but once he was there, he had a good idea who he needed to contact. Then, sending an email to the captain, Sherman Walton, he told them that a new officer was coming to join their ranks and would start on Monday morning. That gave him two days to find himself something to wear, a place to be living, as well as a gun. He would have his own as well as the one they issued. As he'd told Quincey, he'd been a cop before.

By the time the sun came up, he not only had a gun and himself a nice suit, but he had two houses in mind that he would live in. One of them was within walking distance of the station house, the other he would use as his lair. The money that he had stashed all over the state was now in the second home, deep within the walls of the basement. Scott Huff was going to enjoy this...at least he hoped so.

After purchasing a computer, he got back into the email account of Walton. He was a good man, for all appearances, and was worried about someone by the name of Paddy Garrett, the man that he was watching. Whatever was going on with this man was bad. And everything was important.

By backtracking the emails to Walton, he was able to get into the emails of a man by the name of Grant Dudley. He nearly didn't read all the missives from him and his outgoing mail until he found out that the man had been killed recently. He read over some of them, knowing that this would have been a man that he would have had to keep an eye on. But the other names, partners he thought them, would be cops he'd have to befriend. They were into something big, and it seemed that this Garrett person was messing with their plans.

By the time he was ready to rest for the night—being a made vampire, Scott was able to go out during the daylight hours now that he was older—he had a long list of men and women that he was going to look in to. Not all of it was related to Garrett, but some of them were. The station house was on the take, but from who and why, he hadn't been able to find out.

Scott knew that he would, and he'd have information for Quincey too. And now he had to plot and plan. What he was going to do there was anyone's guess, but he'd do it and do it well. Scott didn't realize how much he'd needed this until just today. It was more than he could have hoped for from the vampire. He thought for sure he was just asking to be killed.

The rumors about Quincey were everywhere he went. Some people said that Quincey was a mean bastard. And upon further investigation, those same people had been fucking around and been caught. There were others that thought of him as a humanitarian. Those people had benefited in some way from him.

Then there were the ones that had been helped by him, in some large or small way, and they didn't know anything about him other than his name. Not that he was a vampire, nor that he was older than most buildings in the downtown area. Buildings for the most part that he owned as well.

Scott had never been to Cincinnati. It was a larger city than he thought. There was a big stadium near the river that flowed between it and Kentucky. There were restaurants on nearly every corner, and beautiful works of art that seemed to be a good attraction to most of the people walking around.

Of course, like all major cities, it had its trouble too. Homeless people were sleeping under the bridges and overpasses. There were even some that laid on heating vents from the hotels there. He didn't bother with them for the most part. Whatever they might need or want, it was beyond him to help. Instead, he walked along the riverbank and watched the partiers on the sternwheeler that sat on the edge of the water.

Sitting on the ground, he thought of his life. He really hadn't been kidding when he told Quincey that he'd not been a good man. Some of what he'd done he had justification for. Not very much of it, he'd figured out lately. Like his mercenary work. That had been the darkest period of his life.

Killing for money that he had no use for nor wanted had been his way of making a name for himself. What he had wanted with a name like that, he could no longer remember. But he had a lot of blood on his hands. He supposed he was making up for his children and wife, in some odd way.

"Nay, that isn't right." He looked around and saw that no

one could hear him speaking with himself. He'd not done it for a long time, and thought his inner self might have a better view on himself than his heart did. "You're a bad man and deserve whatever happens to you."

That was true. He did at that. Once he knew that he wanted to die, he'd asked around, trying to find Quincey to have him end his life. Then upon seeing him, he wanted to clear his name, as he'd told him, and go to his long-awaited death with a clear heart. If he even had one anymore that beat with anything but the blackness of his soul.

By sunrise, Scott made his way back to his lair. There was no one there to greet him. No welcoming things that he might have kept for himself over the years. He did touch the locket at his throat, the one that held just a small part of the blankets that he'd wrapped his sons in, as well as a few strands of their hair. Crying softly, hurting for how they'd not lived, Scott closed his eyes and wept until he was ready for sleep. He was sure as he was lying there, talking to himself, that had he been able to do it over, he would have killed his wife and her lover, but he might have made it quicker than he had at the time. Her suffering wasn't anything that he would wish on anyone. He was suffering enough for them both.

~~~

Paddy was having lunch with his sister, Christy, when Jake and Forrest joined them. Christy was laughing at something that he'd said to her, and when Forrest walked by her, he kissed her on the top of the head. Paddy wasn't sure how he felt about that until Forrest explained what he was doing.

"The other day when she was brought here, she smelled of the place that she'd been. I could get her scent, but it was diluted somewhat. Now her scent is her own." Paddy thanked him. "I should have explained before I did it, I'm sorry. But she doesn't know me, and I wasn't sure how she'd feel about being touched. This was harmless, I promise you."

"No, I'm sorry. I shouldn't jump to conclusions. But after what Quincey told me when he got her, I want to find the man and tear him apart all over again." Paddy didn't know what happened to the orderly, but he had an idea that it hadn't been quick. "Christy is trusting. Too much so, sometimes. But she knows about sex, and what to do if someone tries to touch her."

"I kick them in their nuts." Christy laughed when his face heated up. "You are my hero, Paddy Cake. I love you. But you said if I eat all my breakfast, I can go outside and play."

"You can but remember what I told you." Jake told him that there were wolves all around the estate so she'd be fine. "I'll have to find the leader of the pack then. I'm in his territory without permission."

"I spoke to him last night. He came by to tell me that there were people hunting on the property that Jake just purchased. His name is Denny Riggs. He's a good leader, and while his pack is small, they've made a great deal of progress in keeping their pack from leaving for bigger ones." Paddy thanked Forrest. "No problem. I'm just glad that we were able to find you in time, and that Wally helped us with Christy."

There were so many things that he wanted to know about the ghosts and Henry. Mostly why he could see them as well. It hadn't escaped his notice that Wally had called him Henry's mate. Was he? Paddy wasn't sure. The one and only time he'd been close enough to get the other man's scent, there had been something off about it. Now he knew what it was. The scent of death.

Not that he was dying, no, but the fact that he was with the dead. He was well respected in his working to help them. Wally had talked to him about Henry well into the night. For some reason he had come by to tell him what a good man he was, and that he shouldn't be in trouble for the things that had happened where they used to live.

"If you have a secure network here, I'd like to have use of a computer." Jake said that they had a very good network, and that he and Forrest sometimes worked from there. "You two are mates. I'm guessing that is what got you into trouble with your parents?"

"No, my father hated me from the very beginning of my life. And he even went to great lengths to try and get me killed off. Even going so far as to hook me up with a psychopath in hopes that she'd kill me." Paddy laughed when they did. "It's a long and terrible story that eventually got the best woman in the world killed in the process. My grandma. But he's in prison now, and my mom, she killed herself. She'd been suffering from depression for most of her life, and having my dad arrested, it was too much for her."

"He's making it sound as if she wasn't as nutty as the rest of our family. My father hated me as well because I was gay. Didn't bother me so much, what his opinion of me was, but we found out a great many things about both of them the day that it all went to shit." Forrest handed him a key ring with several keys on it. "There is a car in the garage for you to use whenever you need it. And I know that you have been living on your own for some time now. We've decided that should you like to be someplace else, those keys will get you into Jake's former home. It's huge as well, and furnished. There is a staff too, should you decide to go there."

"Why would you do that for me? Not that I don't appreciate it, but why?" They looked at each other, and Paddy felt the hair on his neck rise and his wolf move over him. "What is it? Have you found out something I need to know?"

"A great deal, as a matter of fact, but for now we'd like to explain why we contacted you. My grandma, you see. She was murdered the night my dad was arrested. He killed her. But since Henry's been here — he's our friend — he told us that Grandma had a name that we were to contact for help. That you were the best of the best when it came to sniffing out clues. She was going to hire you on a permanent basis and set you up here, so that she could use your knowledge after this was taken care of with my half-brother."

"I have a job." Both of them shook their head. "What do you mean, no? I do have a job. I'm on the police force in Cincinnati. I've been working there since I was twenty years old. I'm damned good at my job."

"Right now, you're presumed dead. And we're going to let them keep thinking that until we get more information. Quincey, you met him yesterday, he has a man working on the inside that is going to find out just why you were targeted. Is there anyone there that you think you could trust?"

"No, I mean, I really don't know. When I was told about this hit going down, my boss told me." Forrest asked him if it was Walton. "Yes, he's my captain. He told me to go to the take down but not to engage. He said that twice, like he didn't want me hurt. But for all I know.... No, that's not right. He was trying to warn me about something. I just didn't know that I was going to be shot at."

"We don't think he did either. The reason that we know

that is because of some of the emails that have been going back and forth from him to the governor of the state. There is a stupid man, by the way." He was handed some papers that looked like printouts of emails. Forrest told him that they'd been easy to hack in to, and that worried him. "You see, there isn't much of a security system on the police server. Like none at all. And we can't figure out why not."

"Budget cuts. I think that was the first thing to go, Internet. Then when they realized that we couldn't run the station without it, they signed up for the cheapest service they could find. That could be it." Jake seemed to know little about that part, but Forrest agreed with him. "Also, there are some things going on down there that you might not be aware of. You said that there are emails going back and forth between my boss and the governor. What you might have missed is that the governor has a son in the stationhouse that is recruiting. He's trying to get other cops to join his little band of bad guys. They've been in on several robberies, and a few deaths. Nothing has been done about him and the group simply because of who Daddy is."

"I'm assuming that's what got you into trouble." Paddy said that was most of it. "I'm not meaning to pry here, but the more we know, the more we can help you. We brought you here to help us, but I think if we sort of help each other, then we can solve two cases instead of leaving both unsolved."

"You're right. And yes, I'd be glad to help. Wally told me what is going on with the baby. A cutie by the way. And what you two are up against with this Devon guy. You need to find the doctor that performed the tests for a DNA match. And then go from there." He was told that he was dead. "Of course he is. That's what I'd do instead of having a witness.

Also, if this does go to court, I'd demand one, even if you're positive that the other is a fake. Even with proof, you should have another one done. Just to be on the up and up."

"Okay. Like I said, we have a man on the inside helping with your cause. He is to report to us, and we contact Quincey. Quincey's been extremely helpful throughout this whole thing. My grandma, she depended on him a great deal, and they were good friends." Paddy nodded.

Christy moved by the window where they were, her laughter ringing through the open window like a chime on a breezy day. He loved her with all his heart, and knew that they'd have to know a little about her as well.

"My parents are both dead. Christy killed them when she was about nineteen. It wasn't considered murder because she was justified in doing what she'd done. They had abused her in all kinds of horrific ways after she became ill. They didn't want a retarded child — their words, not mine — and had done everything in their power to make sure that she wasn't seen by the public. Since there wasn't the money for a place to put her, they did what they wanted at home." Jake said he was sorry. "So am I. I knew that she was special. Christy is my younger sister by five years. But she only has the mentality of about a six or seven-year-old. She can read and function on her own with minimal supervision, but she scares easily, and as I said, she's too trusting. The place that she was at, it was all I could afford on a cop's salary. I thought she was safe there."

"I'm having the place investigated." Paddy looked at Jake. "I'm discovering when you have all the money you need at your fingertips, you should use it for good. When I was married to Carol, I would never have gotten involved. But now, it's my mission to take care of anyone and everyone that can't do so for themselves."

"Are there others that have been hurt like she would have been?" Jake nodded and looked so sad. "I had no idea. The people that I spoke with that have family in the same place, they had nothing but good things to say about the place. And I did check it out."

"Yes, we're discovering things about that as well. The people that you spoke to are paid to give the place a glowing report. And for everyone that they 'bring in,' they are given a bonus. Like with your sister. The amount of money changes with each person's income. The more they have at their disposal, the more the bonus is." Paddy said that was just sick. "You have no idea. They're not being fed well either. From what we've been able to find out so far, the clients that can speak well, like your sister, they're given about half of what they would need to sustain them for a day. The ones that cannot communicate, they're given crackers and water until they're too weak to move. Then they're catheterized and put on an IV. Out of sight, out of mind, is the philosophy."

"Christ. It sounds like a place my parents would have stuck her. And the amount of money I was paying them, I should have gotten.... Well, you can bet I'm on board with whatever you have up your sleeve." Forrest laughed and said he was suing them, and had forged Paddy's name to the paperwork. "Thank you. If you need me to sign anything else, just let me know."

In the end, not only did he sign off on using them to represent him on the nursing home case, but he took them up on the offer of the other house. He needed to stretch out his wolf, he told them. And he wanted to work with his sister some. She was his only happy spot in this whole world, and he wanted her to know it.

When he was taken to the house, he was overjoyed by what he was being given to use. Not only was a gym on the premises, but also a lot of land. All of it was being watched by the wolf pack, whose pack leader he was introduced to while they were all there.

"I'm only planning to be here for a few weeks. A month at the most." Denny told him he had a job, as his enforcer, if he wanted to stay forever. "I'm honored, sir. I truly am. It'll be something that I think about hard. But I have my sister here, and she's going to need me as well."

"We've been with her. She's a joy to be around." Paddy thanked him for keeping an eye on her for him. "She's been very helpful to the younger pack, just so you know. And since you are here now, with permission, would it be all right with you if she comes to the pack house? You'll see that we have a couple of others that could benefit from her kind of magic. Her happiness will help so many there."

"Yes, but she has a mind of her own. So if you don't want her there all the time, you should let her know right from the start. Otherwise, she'll be asking for a bed." Denny laughed, and told him that would be fine by him as well. "Thank you. My other pack leader, he's got a large pack and has no time so waste on someone like my sister."

"She's not a wolf, is she?" He said that she wasn't, his mom had been wolf but not his father. "Well, that explains it. You both are welcome here anytime. And be assured that we'll keep her safe from any harm."

Glad for the help, not just with Christy but with Jake and Forrest, he settled into his new digs. The land around them would be a wonderful place for his wolf to roam. And to belong to a pack that was so forward thinking was great as well. Paddy thought he might take the man up on his job offer when this was all done. If he didn't go to prison or die first. There was a good possibility that either could happen.

Chapter 5

Devon listened to the man on the other end of the line. He wasn't happy with the things that were going on at the house, but he knew now that he'd opened that can of worms about being an equal heir to the Winslow estate, people would be coming out of the woodwork to help him spend his money.

"I'm not interested in having any kind of investment banker, thank you." The man said he wasn't a banker, but an investor. "I don't care if you're a fucking president of the country, I'm not interested in what it is you're selling me."

Slamming the phone down, he tried to think what he'd been talking about before the phone rang. The man in front of him, a vampire of some age he'd been told, was telling him why it was a mistake to go after Scott.

"You're saying that he's something of a bad guy, correct?" He nodded, his triple chin wobbling like a rooster's neck. "And what makes you think that I'm not a bad guy as well? Someone that could end your life without a care in the world."

"You need me." Devon cocked a brow at him and asked

him how he'd come to that conclusion. "I'm a vampire that can get you anything you desire."

"Anything? Like say, if I wanted you to rob a bank, you could do that?" The vamp disappeared and returned with several bags of what appeared to be money. "You just needed to leave for the blink of an eye and bring me this back? How?"

"I told you, I'm old, and with my age comes certain powers. One of which is the ability to get in and out of tight places without anyone seeing me." He might just keep him around for the simple fact that he'd not have to worry about money for a while. "I can do more than that, too. I have been known to get in and out of a murder scene, one that I created, and no one is the wiser. No witnesses, no nasty DNA to leave behind. Just in and out without any troubles."

Yes, he thought, this was what he needed. Someone to kill off his half-brother and half-sister and be done with them. Because once they were dead, he would be the sole heir of the entire estate without anything coming back to bite him in the ass.

"All right. But this only on a trial basis. I want two more bags of money. And then you'll deliver four every week until I say differently. I don't have to tell you not to hit the same bank all the time, do I?" He said that he'd gotten those from two different banks. "Good deal. And I have the matter of a murder or two that I want you to see to. One of them is a child; you have trouble with that?"

"No, so long as I can have a taste of it before it's dead." Shivering at the thought of what else he might do to this child, he told him he didn't care, so long as it was dead. "Good. I'll do it. Under the assumption that if I do this well, you keep me on as your go to killer. I can feed from them and have some fun."

"You didn't tell me your name." He said he could call him Tom. Whatever the hell that meant. "All right, Tom. When you can get around to killing those two, let me know, without details, when it's done, and we'll go from there. Otherwise, I'm going to kill you where you stand."

"You won't have to worry about that. I've got your back."

When Devon had asked if any of his men knew a vampire, he'd never thought any of them would come through for him. But just today he'd had three approach him, and now he had himself his own hitman. It sounded good.

"Let me get my hitman on that." Laughing, he said something else, just to hear the nice ring to it. "I have someone that can take care of that. Just let me make a call to my hitman."

The thought of Scott being out there and of the trouble he could bring for him still gave Devon nightmares. If the vampire knew just half of what he'd done to ensure that he got the money, the police would be knocking at his door at any moment. But he hadn't told anyone or, and this was what he believed most, Scott was just stabbing in the night about things. That, and the fact that he had only heard of the other vampire, this Quincey person, and for all he knew, the man could be as fake as him being a Winslow.

The rest of his day was spent trying to appease bill collectors. He had the money now, thanks to his hitman, but he knew that he couldn't just go pay cash right away. It would bring the Feds down on him so fast he'd think he had whiplash, and he had been so behind for so long, no one would believe him if he just paid them off. The deal was, he had to make arrangement and stick to them.

Like the electric company. They wanted it all. He couldn't

just say, okay, here it is. They were the worst kind of people to deal with as far as he was concerned. They'd just come out to your house and shut you down without a moment's notice. And the worst part was, then they'd demand a huge fucking deposit before they'd hook it up again. With them, he had a plan.

"I've won a bit of money from the lottery. I'll be down soon, today, to pay the billing off." The lady told him that there would be a five-hundred-dollar deposit made as well. That seemed a bit steep, since he knew they would just use it for something stupid. Or use the interest that would be paid on it while stuck in some account to have a nice party. On his nickel. "Yes, I'll pay that as well. Then you won't shut me off? I have a notice right here that you're doing it between today and tomorrow."

"I'll try and contact the service man on your behalf, but sometimes they don't have good enough phone service to get my calls." He knew she was lying. Devon knew they had better cell service than he did. "You come in and pay the bill, and if he shows up, you can show him your receipt."

Devon didn't bother asking her what would happen if the service man came around while he was gone. She'd just say something like he should have paid his bill on time and he'd not have to worry about that. Or something along those lines.

Hurrying out the door with enough cash to pay his bill and to stop off at the cell service company and pay that as well, Devon decided that he was going to have him a nice meal out. Steak and potatoes. He'd had enough of bologna and cheese on crackers to last him a lifetime.

The people at the office of the electric company assured him that his house was safe. Just to be sure, he went by there to see. He had paid his cell service too, and was told he could upgrade now. Taking advantage of the deal there, he got the newest phone and unlimited everything. He was nearly dancing when he entered the restaurant to have dinner.

Devon was trying his best to be smart with his windfall. He hadn't counted it as yet; the first bag of cash had been all hundreds, wrapped up in nice little bands that said how much was in there. After counting that bag, he knew that he'd be set for a long while. At least until his next bags came in. Then he thought of the money from the Winslow estate.

Did he really want it now? Oh, hell yeah, he wanted it. He might not deserve it, but he wanted it. It was going to go a long way in setting him up in life. Not just with the money, but the prestige that his father had. Jacob Winslow might not have been his real father, but Devon was going to be just like him, in every way that he could. Also, he thought that having women fawning all over him all the time would be a great perk.

Devon knew what he looked like. Short in stature, he wasn't what women thought of as a manly man. He had a small dick too, which he knew how to use when he was able to get laid…which wasn't as often as he wanted. Women laughed at him, and that pissed him off. And thanks to whoever had sired him, he was going bald. But money would take care of all that, and anything else that he wanted. Money spoke.

After enjoying a fine meal, probably made finer by the fact that he knew that he'd be going out a lot more now, he walked home. He wanted a car, one that said I fucking have money, but he had to be safe rather than sorry. Besides, he needed to get rid of some of the belly fat he'd put on now that he was going to be rich. And he'd be the richest man alive soon.

His home was dark when he arrived, and he was sure that they'd turned his power off anyway. But going inside and turning on the first switch that he came to, he was relieved when it came on. Devon wasn't sure what he would have done about it this late at night, but someone would have paid. They might yet.

Now all he had to do was wait to be told that his poor brother was dead, as well as his sister. There would be a period of mourning, he supposed. Even though he didn't know either of them, he would make an appearance. Standing in front of his bathroom mirror, he started practicing his sad face.

In the end he had himself laughing so hard that he had to sit down. The sad face was stupid looking, and he knew that anyone could see it. So he started practicing his thrilled face, and that got him giggling. He knew that he sounded like a mad man, but at this point there was no one around, and he was having fun. The pressures of having no money to speak of had been lifted off his shoulders, and he was enjoying things. He wondered how he'd celebrate when he had the Winslow estate.

Sometime after midnight he fell into bed. Tomorrow was going to be a big day for him. His family would be dead, and he'd be rich. He wished that he'd gotten some sort of time frame from Tom, but he'd been so excited to have the cash that he'd forgotten to ask.

Devon woke up sitting straight up in the bed. Something had awakened him, and he hadn't any idea what it might have been. His first thoughts were that Scott had come back to get him. Then he dismissed that idea when he didn't hear anyone around. Turning on the lights, he thought for sure that the robe at the bottom of his bed had moved.

Curling up as tightly as he could at the headboard, Devon called out to whoever was there that he had a gun. He screamed when the said gun was dropped on the bed in front of him, then the six bullets that had been in it dropped one at a time.

"Who's there? What do you want?" The robe moved again, this time to the floor. But before he could peek to where it might have gone, it rose up and looked as if something...no, someone...was wearing it. "Please, don't hurt me."

The scratching, like the sound of nails on a chalkboard, had him looking at the window. His heart was racing now, and he was suddenly freezing to death. But he dared not reach for anything. Devon was terrified that whatever sort of ghost this was, or whatever it was, they'd think he was reaching for the gun.

The scratching continued, and then he saw what had been scratched in his glass. KILLER. Devon asked whatever was with him—he wasn't ready to believe it was actually a ghost—what they wanted of him.

The sound was low, eerily like a cat that needed to be killed. When he asked what it had said, he heard it as plain as day. "Dead."

"You want me dead? What have I done to you that you'd wish something like that on me? Come out where I can see you. You owe me that much for scaring me half to death." He wasn't keen on using that word, but he knew he had to make a point. "Come out here. Show yourself."

Devon wasn't sure that he really wanted to see whatever it was. He felt the coldness as it seeped into his bones. He had a feeling that no matter how many blankets he had to pull over himself, he'd never be warm again. Then he saw it. The robe dropped, and he screamed over and over.

His mom was there, and she looked just like the day he'd murdered her. Her face was smashed up and her body broken, like it was when he'd shoved her into the path of an oncoming truck, and she'd finally landed several feet away.

Hitting his head on the back of his bed, he knew that he was going to die. And it wasn't fair, he thought as the ghost of his mom flew around the room. When it came at him, her body going through his, Devon let the terror of the night take him under and slipped into unconsciousness.

~~~

Henry stood on the front porch for five minutes. Debating with himself whether or not to ring the doorbell, the giggle of someone close alerted him that he wasn't alone. Turning toward the sound, he was embarrassed to see Christy sitting on the swing rocking back and forth.

"You talk to yourself." He nodded and asked if her brother was home. "Yes, but he's sleeping. I had a bad dream last night and he stayed with me. Are you going to sit down and talk to me? I won't hurt you. I have stuff to drink too."

"Yes, of course." She offered him a glass of water. She had several of them on a tray, all of them mismatched, but he was charmed by her thoughtfulness. "How are you enjoying living here? It's a very lovely home, I've been told."

"It is pretty. And has lots of places I can play in too. Paddy Cake gave me a computer of my very own." She handed him the small handheld device. "I like playing games on it, but Paddy Cake said that I have to read on it too. I like to read, but playing games is much more fun, don't you think?"

"I love to read, myself. A book though. I've never been very good with things that are electronic." She nodded, and he started to rock in the wicker chair he was sitting in. "I was trying to figure out if I wanted to talk to your brother or not. I'm not sure this is right."

"He's always right. I asked him if that was true, and he told me that it was. But he told me later that he was just kidding me. But I don't care. To me, he's perfect. I'm glad to be here with him too. That other place, they were mean to me, and they wanted to touch me." Henry told her he was very sorry about that, and took a sip of his water. But he nearly choked on it…it was sugar water, and very sweet. Her innocent laughter had him laughing as well. "I'm not allowed to have pop. But I can have water. It's not as good, but I like it."

"I don't think Paddy would be any happier with you drinking sugar water." She smiled at him. "You're a beautiful young woman. You remind me of my little sister when she was alive."

"I'm alive." He said that he could see that. "When I was a little girl, I killed my mom and dad. They were hurting me. So when they let me loose to go to the back yard to pee, I grabbed a stick and I hit them over the head with it a lot of times. They can't hurt me anymore. Hello, Paddy Cake."

He looked up at the man standing there without a shirt on. It was the first time that he'd seen him since he'd been hurt, and without bandages. Standing up, all Henry could do was stare at him.

Paddy looked like he'd been carved from stone. He had a tapered waist, and abs that looked like he lifted boulders for fun. His hair was mussed, some of it hanging down over his tawny eyes. The growth of what he assumed was day old beard made him look delicious and charming at the same time.

"He wants to talk to you about something. And I was entertaining him."

Paddy thanked her, but he kept staring at Henry. Swallowing twice, Henry said that he needed to go. "Don't. I need to talk to you as well. If you don't mind."

"This was a bad idea. I really should go." Paddy came all the way out of the house and he had to look away. "I don't want to be rude...I know this is your home and all, but could you go get dressed? Please?"

Soft laughter, this time from Paddy. "What part of me bothers you, Henry?" He moved closer and Henry backed up. "This conversation, it wouldn't have to do with the fact that you're my mate, would it?"

"I'm gay. I shouldn't have come here. I should have—" Paddy said that he was too. "What? What did you just say? There isn't any way that you're gay too."

"Oh, but I am." With that, he pulled him back into the house and kissed him. "Oh, Henry, I was so afraid that you'd turn me down."

The kiss was devastating and hungry. Henry touched his chest, felt the heat of it, the smooth muscles, and he fell in love. There was nothing keeping him from exploring his body, his neck and his mouth. When Paddy pulled away, stepping back from him, Henry whimpered.

"My sister. I have to talk to her." Henry nodded and realized that his shirt was undone, his belt was gone. Leaning over to pick it up to put it back, Paddy stopped him with his hand to his chest. "Don't do that. I just got them off. I just have to tell Christy something. I'll be back."

Henry leaned against the wall, holding his belt like a lifeline. He heard Paddy talking to Christy, asking her if she wanted to go to the pack house, they were having ice cream. Her delighted squeal made Henry smile, and he closed his eyes listening to the two of them.

"You have to wait on Beth. She's coming as her wolf. When she gets here, you can go with her, okay?" She told him she'd be good. "I know you will, honey. You have a wonderful time, and when you come back, we'll watch some television."

"Can I stay all night? I can make sure that Beth is okay with that. Can I, Paddy Cake?" He told her he'd have to find out. "Can you ask her daddy? He likes me."

"Everyone likes you." There was a lull in their conversation, and then Paddy spoke again. "Denny said that he doesn't mind and that you don't have to bring anything to put on. You can wear some of Beth's things. Look, Christy, she's there now. Have fun."

When he came back into the house, he shut the door this time. And when the lock turned, it sounded very loud in the large foyer. Henry couldn't breathe. It was as if he was being strangled by the pressure…no, the tension in the room. But as soon as Paddy touched him, a gentle touch to his cheek, he calmed down.

"Why does she call you Paddy Cake?" He felt his face heat up and shook his head. "I'm sorry. I don't know what's wrong with me. It's like there isn't a filter between my mouth and my head."

"It's fine. We need to start over in this, but slower. Not too slow, but slower. I'm nervous as well. I've never had a mate before. And when you told me…. Anyway, when Christy was little and would get to see me, she had trouble saying Patrick. I told her it was like patty cake, the nursery rhyme that she had been learning. She's called me that since. I don't think anyone has ever asked me that before."

"I'm sorry." Paddy told him to stop saying that, they were fine. "Yes, I guess we are. I was coming over here to talk to you. I haven't any idea what my plan was to tell you, but just to, I guess, find out what you knew, if anything. Wally told me."

"I heard him. I wasn't sure what to think about it then. So I started avoiding you. I had no idea that you were gay as well." They entered the large kitchen, and Paddy started pulling things from the fridge. "I haven't been very open about it. Mostly because of what I do. Gay cops don't last long in the precinct I was in. I didn't share, and no one asked. I'm not sure, but I think a few of them had guessed. But for the most part, they kept their opinions to themselves. I'm making us some dinner. I need to do something before I take you to the floor."

Without comment, not sure what he'd say, Henry sat on the stool near where Paddy was working. He thought about life with this man, and decided that he could do this. Be happy with him. Provided his life didn't mess it up for him.

"I'm an actor." Paddy laughed and told him that Christy had told him. "She's seen my movies? I don't know if that's good or bad."

"The ghost, I think he told her." Henry asked about that. "I think that I can see them because of our relationship. That was another clue that we were mates. But I think Christy can see them because she's child-like. Wally came by to tell me that he's hung around with you, and had all your life.

Explained a few things to me as well. He wondered if that would be an issue."

"Is it?" Paddy shook his head and handed him a thick sandwich. "I don't usually eat this much. I mean, the camera adds ten pounds."

"You're going to burn it off." He nearly swallowed too fast. When Paddy sat down and dug into his food, Henry did the same. They talked around bites and got to know each other. "I'm not going to be able to go back to that precinct. I've already come to that conclusion. They're dirty there, and I'd just as soon not go down with them when it happens. Because I'm going to make sure that it does."

"I'm done as an actor as well. There were some pictures that came out…untrue, but they were damaging enough. I never made a secret of what I was…a gay man acting in a romantic setting. But once it came out, you'd think that I had pulled the wool over everyone's eyes and become a gay man just to piss people off." They both laughed. "My mom died right in the middle of all that. Not because of it…she'd been sick for some time, and we knew it was going to happen. But when I got the call from Forrest to come here and help them out, I was sitting in my bedroom contemplating just killing myself."

"I'm glad that you didn't." Henry nodded. "I would imagine that it was difficult, even with you being up front with people. I never took the chance. It wasn't as if I regretted my decision, but I think it was safer for me to do that. I had no one to lean on when things got bad. And they were for a long time after my parents were gone. Christy too far away for me to visit, even if I would have been allowed. It came out later that she was justified in her actions. It made it no less hard on her, but at least she didn't end up staying in a prison mental institution. Although, it sounds like she didn't get any better treatment where she was either."

"I'm charmed by her. She's funny and kind. And very honest. Oh, she drinks sugar water, did you know that?" He said that he didn't. "I was told she couldn't have pop, so she improvised a little. When she offered me something to drink, I expected something like tepid water. I nearly strangled when I swallowed the sweetest water I've ever drank."

When they were finished eating, they cleaned up their mess. Paddy told him that their cook would be coming in to work full time tomorrow, and that Christy went to the pack house for lessons every day. She was smart, he told him, but she needed to have things reinforced. They made their way to the living room to sit down.

"That means we have the entire night to get to know each other. And there doesn't have to be any sex, not right away." Henry smiled. "Yeah, it sounded much better in my head. Like I was trying to be this great guy. Anyway, I'd like for you to move in here with us. It's not my home, but since neither of us have anything to go back to where we lived before, I think we should find us a place to stay here. I like Forrest and Jake, and I think you do as well. But it would have to be much smaller than this place. I'm probably not going to be getting any more checks."

"I have money. Not as much as the other two do, but I've done well for myself. I always knew that someday I'd be finished, just not this soon, so I saved and didn't spend on a great many things. A house that'll sell for more than I paid for it. So we can go bigger, but not like this, as you said."

They didn't make any plans, not long term anyway. Paddy

told him about his life as a cop, and Henry told him about some of the things he'd had to do as an actor. And about his mom. They were sitting side by side on the couch, and when Paddy put his head on his shoulder, Henry felt better. Neither of them had a shirt on still, and when Paddy leaned over and took his nipple into his mouth, Henry held him to him as he reached for his cock.

Things going slow, my ass, he thought. The need between the two of them was palpable. He could feel it along his skin. Henry shifted on the couch and ended up on his back, with Paddy over him. He kissed his flesh, licked his navel. Everywhere he touched him, it was like being seared with a blade. And when Paddy pulled his pants open, Henry helped him.

Being naked had never been an issue for him, but Henry felt exposed now. He wondered if Paddy would be disappointed in his body. Would he find the little bit of belly that he'd put on since his mom died disgusting? When he looked at him, Henry felt all his insecurities disappear and he smiled at him.

"You're thinking much too hard." He nodded. "I am going to make you cum so hard that you're going to feel like your head has exploded."

"I need you, Paddy." He kissed his cock through his boxers. "Christ, I'm not going to last long."

"Good. Then we can rest up for the next round."

His boxers were torn away; Henry wasn't afraid when Paddy's hands morphed into claws. Even the small cut to his hip was erotic. And when he took his cock into his mouth, Henry cried out. Christ, he really wasn't going to last long.

Chapter 6

Paddy loved being touched. It was the wolf in him that brought it out for him. And when Henry put his hand on his head, it was all he could do not to howl his approval. But he wanted this man in a way that he'd never experienced before.

He loved the way he tasted, the sounds that he made when he was excited. Paddy wanted him to do more, to make more sounds. To taste more of him. Moving his mouth down to his thigh, he found a ticklish place there. Henry's knees were scarred with small wounds. Kissing each one of them, it brought him to his calves, the back of his legs.

"You're killing me." Paddy laughed as he sat up on his knees. Pulling Henry's foot into his hands, he massaged the tightness of it, kissed his ankle as he softened the muscles. "You do that well. I'm not sure anyone has ever touched my feet before."

"I love to touch." Henry said that he did as well. And when he sat up, pulling him to him, Paddy gave him as much as the kiss was taking. Love. This was what love was like.

"Roll over, I want to touch your back."

It wasn't as simple as it sounded. They were both large men, tall and wide with muscle. When Henry ended up on the floor, he followed him, sitting on his hips and rubbing his hands hard over him from ass to shoulder. Kissing him when he got the chance, he loved the way his flesh tasted when it was warmed up.

"I need you." Paddy told him to be patient. They had their whole lives ahead of them. "Yeah, but you're going to be sorely disappointed when I die from need right now."

They had fun with their love making, touching and joking. It was both sexy and relaxing. Paddy wanted to take his time, but Henry was in a hurry. When Paddy was flipped over onto his back, he looked up at the man he would spend the rest of his life with and told him that he loved him.

"And I love you as well. I think I have since I first met you." Henry entered him slowly, stretching him so that there'd be no pain. When he was seated as far as he could go, Paddy cried out when he started to move. Touching his cock with his own hands, the two of them came hard, their bodies bowed up from the floor and each other as cum spread over both their bodies.

When Henry dropped over him, he held him tightly. Paddy wasn't an emotional person before or after sex, but he felt his eyes fill when he thought of them together. They had a lot to work out, things to make right, but he knew that for the rest of his days there would always be someone there for him to lean on and to talk to.

"When I was a kid, I must have been about ten or so, my mom sat me down and explained sex to me. It wasn't until I was older that I realized she'd not done it as other adults would…she explained to me about sex between two people, two men." Paddy asked him if he'd known back then. "Yes, but I had no idea that she did. And she continued to support me, encouraging me to be what I was and not to hide behind anything. So when she died, I felt as if I had no one, and that I never would."

"You have me." Henry looked at him and rolled to his back too. "My parents knew that I was a homo; their words, not mine. When I was seventeen, I was sick of changing the name of the person I was seeing. Dating girls that meant nothing to me. And worst of all, they were forever blaming me and what I was for everything that happened to them. Even how Christy was born."

"What happened with her?" Paddy looked at Henry, trying to think how to tell him. "I'm sorry. I made it sound like she was hurt and that someone did it. Was it a birth defect or something?"

"No, she was hurt. My mom did it. When Christy was an infant, she was considered to be in the high end of the spectrum of weight and height. My dad wasn't tall, neither was Mom, but she worried that Christy would be a freak of nature. So she started giving her home remedies to make her have bowel movements to take some of the weight away." Henry said he was sorry for that. "Yes, well, whatever it was, it affected her brain. Her noodle, she calls it. And before she was five years old, she started slowing down in her ability to learn even the simplest of tasks. It wasn't until she was fifteen and they sent her way that she started to get better. By then, the developmental part of her brain was ruined."

They got up and pulled their pants on. Henry said that he needed to let Jake and Forrest know that he'd not be home tonight, and Paddy asked again if he'd live there. Henry seemed to hesitate, and Paddy was hurt by that.

"You don't have to. I understand." Henry asked him what he meant by that. "You know, you're a big-time actor, and I'm nothing but a lowly cop on a cop's pay. I understand if you'd rather stay with the rich guys."

"Hang on just one fucking moment. You think...? Well of course you do. You think that I'm hesitating because of your fixation on money. No. I was worried about your sister. And how a sudden change might affect her. I love her too, like my own sister, and you.... What the fuck is wrong with you?" Paddy felt stupid. He was hurt and had taken it out on his lover. Before he could tell him how sorry he was, Henry continued. "You think this is an easy decision for me? It's not. I don't want to take you down with me. I have newspapers looking for me, even now, to get the lowdown on my life. How I'm a gay man playing a part that is so not me. Even though I have said right from the first that I'm not a heterosexual man, they are all forgetting that in order to sell papers and those rags they print up that're in the grocery line."

Paddy kissed him. Hard and quick. When Henry started to speak again, Paddy kissed him again, this time showing him how sorry he was, how much he loved him. Then when he pulled away from him, he pressed his forehead to his and felt the tears fall along his cheeks.

"I'm a fool. A terrified, stupid fool." Henry said he wasn't going to disagree with that. Laughing, he looked up at him. "I'm not sure where that all came from. I'm usually not so insecure. But today, with you, all I can think about is finding love and then it being taken from me."

"I'm not leaving. And if you'd like to start over, I'll tell you, I don't want your sister to be hurt or feel left out because I'm here." Paddy nodded, and told him he didn't know how she'd react either. "You've never had a live in? Not at all?"

"No, I never have. When I needed sex, which after a while seemed to diminish a lot, I would go away for it. Like a few towns over. I was careful, as I said. And as for having someone over with my sister here, she's not lived with me since I was a teenager." Paddy sat down on the couch again and hoped that Henry would sit with him. When he did, Paddy told him again how sorry he was.

"We have a lot to learn about each other. I mean, when I first came over here, I was ready to have you pull your gun and blow my head off." Paddy said he didn't work that way. "Oh yeah, you have other means of disposing of bodies?"

"Yes, I let the wolf pack have them." They were both laughing when the phone rang. Paddy hadn't been answering it since it wasn't his home. But when Henry got up and took the call, he watched him sit behind the desk to take notes. It was for Jake, he mouthed to him.

"Yes, I have it here. The phone number as well." He wrote down that it was DNA test results on Jenna. "Yes, I understand that you can't give those to me. I'll give him the message as soon as we hang up. I would imagine that he'll be calling you right back."

He called Jake next. The ease with which he did this made Paddy think that he was an organized man. Liked things in their place, and those places were labeled. Paddy was organized to a point, but he was more of a shove it in a box and hope he remembered where he'd put it sort of organized person. Like his Christmas things…they were in a box and all in one place, but he was sure that his tree was in three different boxes, with ornaments sprinkled around them.

"He wants us to come over before he calls them. Forrest isn't home...he went to get diapers and stuff. Jake wants us to wait with him until he comes back. I told him that I'd ask you." Paddy said it would take them a little bit to get cleaned up. "Okay, I'll tell him."

When he hung up the phone, they went to the bedroom that they'd be sharing. He didn't have enough clothing to fill the giant closet that was in the room. Nor the two dressers. He might have to take a trip to his apartment sometime. But in the meantime, he'd have to get him a few things. He wasn't even sure where to go shopping without being caught out.

In ten minutes they were on their way. They'd taken a shower together, and Paddy had scrubbed Henry's back. But knowing that they were on a time limit now, they hurried through getting dressed. By the time they were at the other house, Forrest had returned, and Jenna was crying.

Paddy didn't know a great deal about children that was good. In dealing with the public he'd seen all kinds of kids, from troubled to being drugged up and killed. When he was handed the little girl, she stared up at him like he was something strange. He started talking to her in a calm voice until she went to sleep in his arms.

"You're really good at that. She's been upset for the last ten minutes. I think she felt my stress when I was trying to feed her." Paddy sat down like he was sitting on raw eggs. "Something that I've learned, they're not breakable. I mean, she's tiny, but she's really bendable."

"Bendable? What have you been doing to her, making her into a pretzel?" They all laughed, and that was what was needed to break the tension about the call. Forrest said that they were all there, so go ahead with the call. It was the longest call being made that he'd ever witnessed.

He told the lady who he was, and the number he'd been given at the hospital that was his code to get the information. When he sat down hard at the desk and closed his eyes, Paddy knew that the results were not what they were hoping for. When Forrest went to Jake and held his hand, Jake nodded up at him.

"She's my half-sister. There isn't any doubt about it now." They all congratulated them both as Jake continued. "The autopsy is back on Stacy, her mom, and she died of congestive heart failure. They didn't know that when she'd been in to see the doctors, and it was just too much for her when she went into labor. Also, the doctor said he thought that she'd not had the will to live. That knowing her baby was going to be safe was enough for her. She left us a letter, and he's forwarding it on to us today."

"Now what do we have to do? I mean, Devon is still out there, right? You don't think he's going to give up now that it's confirmed that she's related to you, is he?" Jake said he didn't expect him to. "All right. This is what I'd do. I'd call him out. Tell him that you're willing to part with some of the money—not all, but a portion of it—if there is a second test done. I have to tell you guys, I think he's full of shit. Your dad was fucking his mom, and he figured that he'd get some cash for it."

"And what if he is my half-brother? Then what do I do?" Paddy shrugged and said he'd pay him about a tenth of what he got. "You have any idea how much that is? I mean, seriously. It's still going to be about a billion bucks. And you know what? He's not going to be satisfied with that either."

"Christ, you guys are wealthy, aren't you? I mean, I knew you had money, but Christ oh mighty. One tenth is going to be a billion dollars?" Paddy sat down and then put his head between his knees. "Christ."

"I'm sorry." He asked Jake why he was sorry. "Because I've upset you. I shouldn't have been so harsh either. That's not like me. And no, it's not going to be enough for him either. I know that. Nor do I believe that he's related to me. I think even Grandma knew that. But this guy isn't going to just take the money and go away, is he?"

Paddy shook his head as he sat up. "You have to get him first in this. I don't mean kill him. You do that, and you'd be the first person on my list of suspects. No, you have to get him where it counts most, and obviously that's going to be his pocket."

"How? I'm sure you have a plan. What do you think we should do? Because at this point, I'm willing to do just about anything." Paddy said he wasn't sure he was going to like it. "Probably not, but this is my family here, my mate, my little sister. As my grandma used to say, you fuck with what is mine, you take on the worst of me. And in my family, I include you and Henry too. I'm glad you two have come together as a couple."

"Thank you. And so are we." Paddy looked at Henry. "You wanna get dirty with me and the boys here?"

Laughing, Henry said he was willing to do anything to or with him. Embarrassed at how it was turned around on him, Paddy said he needed information and he sat at the computer. This was war. He had a family, and they were going to win this sucker.

~~~

Scott couldn't believe how bad this station was. Not only was just about everyone taking a cut of what was brought in, they barely did more than what was required of them in an eight-hour shift. And the few that were out doing the job were so stressed out and overworked that he wasn't sure they were going to be honest much longer. The only holdout that he'd met so far to all this seemed to be the captain, and he wasn't having an easy time of it either.

Reaching out with his mind again, he gathered as much information as he could find. Walton was taking the money offered him, but every penny of it was going into a safety deposit box at his bank. He'd not even taken any from it when his daughter had needed a little extra to get her through the next month. He'd just handed over his lunch allowance he put out for himself, and told her that's all he had.

That didn't make him any less of a crook than the rest of them, it just made him stronger in some way. Scott wrote it all down in the little book he'd been carrying around. He was careful not to let anyone see him with the book, always pulling shadows and magic around him when he did. And he hid it on his body in a way that the only way to find it was to cut him up. Not going to happen either.

When Quincey appeared in the room with him, he knew that no one else could see the man and left the office, pulling out a pack of cigarettes as he went. This no smoking in the buildings was helping him a great deal. It was something that he'd done the other times when he showed up.

"They have an idea where he is." Quincey asked him how they'd figured it out. "Cameras. There is one across the street from the parking garage where he was picked up. They only have a partial plate...they found it before I could take care of all of it. I've only managed to slow them down, but they're going to find him soon enough. Can you warn them?"

"Yes, I can do that. What of the captain here. Is he in with them?" Scott explained what he'd found out. "You think he's being pressured into taking the money for some reason? Blackmail over something?"

"Could be. I never thought of that. I can dig deeper into his head. He has a daughter who's struggling a great deal through no fault of her own. I'd like to take care of her boss, if you'd not mind." Quincey asked what was going on. "He's a pervert, and wants her to be his plaything so she can have more hours. So far she's been able to keep him away, but she's behind in her rent and utilities. I think he has it in his head that since she had a kid without being married and is on her own, she'd be all right with him taking her over the table. Walton won't step in because this boss is in with the crew here. And he's worried that it'll cause her more trouble, or worse."

"Have they talked about the young man?" Another person came out to smoke, and talking was cut off between the two of them. Quincey whispered, just above the sound of a breeze going through a tree, but Scott heard him. "I would like for you to let me take your blood, please. It would be much safer for you and myself as well. You don't have to; the amount of information that you've given me on this makes me believe that you have turned a new leaf."

Nodding, he let his beast go for a moment, just enough for his hand to turn into a claw. Cutting his hand with it, he acted like he'd done it on the railing around them. The other cop came to look while Quincey took his wound to his mouth. It was over in seconds, but it was enough time for them to make a connection.

What about the young man, Patrick? Anything on him? Scott told him what he'd been able to find out, none of it good. *So, he's been finding their shipments and play rooms and busting them. That's a good start, I would say. And they're blaming him for the deaths of the others? The innocent men as well?*

Yes. Two days ago there were fingerprints found on the guns that the other men used. Since I knew that he had nothing to do with their deaths, only to defend himself, someone wants him dead bad. Then this morning, a video came up that shows Garrett running from the scene of the crime. I think he was running, but it was from the ones shooting him. Quincey asked if he knew where this information was coming from. *The governor. He is telling the news that he pulled some strings and got some of the wonderful citizens in that area to release their tapes to him. He said that he had to assure then that the police wouldn't hold it against them for turning them in. That was why it had taken them so long.*

I have a feeling that once they find Patrick, they're not going to wait for him to confess nor turn himself in. He's going to be dead the moment they find him. Scott agreed, and told him that whoever he was with, they'd be just as dead. *Yes, I think you are correct on that as well. Now what, I wonder? Do I just kill the lot of them? Patrick has found his mate and they're very happy now. But they know this is hanging over their heads. Also, there is the trouble with Devon; I refuse to call him a Winslow. Too many things are connected here for me to know which problem to take care of first.*

This one isn't going anywhere until they find him. I think I've put up enough road blocks, for now anyway, that it'll be at least a few more days. And Devon has a weak spot. It's money. I know that sounds like everyone's spot, but he will do just about anything for money in his pocket. He's been without for too long. Quincey asked if he meant paying him off. *No, I don't think that'll work with him. But it could be used to lure him out of his home, long enough for someone to get in and get something that will give the others a heads up on whether or not he's really related. It would go a long way, to me, knowing that whatever bullshit he is slinging, it's not going to hit them.*

I like that idea. But what if he won a nice dinner? Something that when he walks away from his meal, we can pick up and use. You know that whatever is left behind is no longer his, like trash or his DNA on a glass. I saw that once, I believe. Scott laughed to himself, and asked how much television he actually watched. *None if I can get around it. But sometimes, women have it on in the background.*

Scott didn't ask. He didn't want to know anything personal about this man. It was scary enough to be working with him, much less knowing too much about him. Quincey said that he'd take care that the man won his dinner. He would also make sure that there were people in place to make sure that it was done correctly.

Not that I think it'll end up in a court of law, the way we're doing this, but there is no reason to take a chance that he may well be related to them. Quincey looked around the office that they'd come back to when it was no longer necessary for them to talk outside. *Something will need to be done about this place. And very soon. They are hurting a great many people by not doing their jobs properly. You think on that, and let me know your ideas on getting things back to being right. And about the governor as well. He is running the state, and if it continues to work well here for him, then there is no telling how widespread this will become soon.*

After Quincey left him, Scott worked on the reports that he'd been assigned. He was on desk duty for the next three weeks due to an injury that he'd gotten two days after starting. Scott had been coming out of the showers when someone hit him from behind.

He knew who it had been; he smelled the man as soon as he came up behind him. But he didn't regret letting him get away with it for now. Scott was doing just what he needed to do to help out Quincey and the others.

However, he was reasonably sure that the rookie would never do that again, if he ever got out of traction where he could move his arms without screaming. Scott hadn't done it to the man, but he was sure that Quincey had either done it or had someone do it. Scott had been in the hospital on a gurney when the man suddenly found himself in a great deal of pain.

While he pretended to read over the report that he was correcting, he reached out to the few men that were in the station. There should have been forty that showed up for work today, but so far he'd only counted ten. And of them, only two had gone out to work. The rest were playing on their phone, their computer, or simply sleeping.

He nearly skipped over the man who was watching porn on his computer. But Scott realized right away that it was what he was doing under the desk that was important. As he read his mind on what he was doing, he contacted Quincey to let him know. This would be important to a lot of people.

They're going to have a pick-up of guns and drugs in the morning at the pier near the sternwheeler. There will be seventeen men from the force there, as well as the governor. Quincey asked if he had a name on the container. *Yes, and I have a number on it as well. There will be cars on another container, and those are being driven straight to the governor's vacation home. Which is in West Virginia.*

Scott gave him the information on both containers, along with the address of the governor. *I'm not going to hit them while they're on the water, but I will have someone follow the cars to the house. Then once that is taken care of, the rest will hit the container. Good work.* Scott thanked him, but paused. *What else?*

Women. There are women inside the one with the cars. Not willingly either. They're entertainment for the party that's being given by the governor in celebration of his upcoming election. They've not voted.... He's got someone working the polls for him to win. Christ, this is much deeper and more sinister than I thought. He's using the names of dead people, nothing new there, to vote for him. And however much more he needs to win, that's what they're going to use, plus more. Quincey said that the party would be a perfect place for him to take care of this. *Just...I don't know, be careful. These men are playing for keeps, and stand to get a great deal of money from the stuff that is coming in.*

I will. And thanks. Remember what I told you, Scott. If you're questioned, you just leave it to me. Nothing comes from your mouth, all right? He said he'd be a mute if they asked. *Good. I can't cover what I don't know. Just do what you're doing, be careful, and let me handle this from now on. You did a great job. Now we're going to get this guy where it hurts, and Patrick will be just fine.*

Too bad you can't have him in on this. Quincey didn't say anything. *You think you can swing that? I mean, this guy has had a shitty thing pasted to his name. It would be nice if he could get revenge like this.*

You don't wish for the credit? Scott told him that he didn't. *Not ever. Thank you, my friend. Yes, I'll see what I can do for Patrick.*

Scott continued to listen to the men in the office but returned to the cop he'd dubbed Porno several times during the shift. He was making all sorts of plans, and on his phone. If only he could get that sucker, he knew that it would go a long way in helping out with this case. But he wasn't going to do anything stupid. He had a lot riding on this, mostly his reputation, and he wanted that back. More than he wanted to live, he thought.

Chapter 7

Paddy didn't like this. He knew that anything could and would go wrong at any time. The party he was near was going full swing, and there still weren't any sightings of the cargo. He looked over at the agent that was with him and told him he was sorry it was taking so long.

"Not me. This is perfect." Paddy asked him what he meant. "We've been trying to get this guy for nearly six years, and you helped us more than you know. We have a cargo container full of drugs in a warehouse with seventy or so agents watching them unload it. There is a bill of sale with it that has the governor's name on it. That's enough to get him on. But the women and the cars? Just icing on the cake. You did a great job. And we'll get the other cleaned up for you as well. Good thing you had your body cam on you."

"Yes, I think of that every day." The small device in his ear buzzed and he waited for someone on the other end to tell him nothing was coming. But when he heard the route the container was coming from, he told the agent. "They're about ten minutes out. You guys are in charge of this, but I'd really like to be there when you take him down."

"We're not taking him down." Paddy just stared at him. This could not be happening to him. "You're doing it. I know that it's not in your jurisdiction, but for this, we're going to make an exception. Once you have him cuffed, we'll take him in. It's the least we can do for you in all this."

"Thank you." Agent Garth shook his hand and told him thanks. "I just couldn't take it any longer. The way they were working the streets and such."

"And being accused of murder for a crime you didn't commit didn't help either." He laughed, and they heard the squawk of Garth's radio. "We're circling the property now. If anyone approaches you after we hit the party, you just refer them to me. All right? I don't want you arrested too. And as soon as they have my go ahead, they're going into the station house and taking it, as well as the cargo full of drugs and guns. Just don't get hurt."

They were in the perfect position to see not just the cargo coming in, but the governor having the time of his life as well. They were afraid at first that he'd not be at his own party, but he'd shown up about an hour ago with not only his mistress, but also most of the police force. Most of which, he'd been told, were on duty and shouldn't have been here. Paddy reached out to Henry and asked him how he was doing.

Fine. This is amazing, isn't it? It's almost too good to be true. And being a waiter to take the order of the other moron that fucked around with our new family is like having my cake and eating you as well. He laughed and felt better for it. *The man has no taste in food. He can have anything on the menu that he wants, and he and his date are having no appetizers, and no side dishes. I swear, some*

100

people are just plain dumb.

What would you have if we were to have dinner at the same place? Henry told him that he'd have the grilled salmon with the grilled asparagus. A dinner salad, as well as the garlic mashed potatoes. *Been studying the menu, have you?*

Yes, of course. I was thinking that when this is done, we should come here. With Jake, Forrest, and your sister. It would be a blast. Paddy was happy that he liked to include Christy in everything they did. *How much longer do you think you'll be? Not rushing you, but Jake invited us over to dinner tonight and I wasn't sure you were going to make it.*

I won't. I have to fill out some paperwork here and then drive home, depending on how late it is. Henry told him to stay in a hotel, that way he'd not worry about him driving so late. *I might just do that. I have the credit cards that you gave me. I've not been sleeping well. Someone is keeping me awake.*

They were laughing when he saw the cargo, and told Henry that he'd talk to him after it was done. When the connection closed, he felt him touch his mind again and was told that he and Christy loved him. It made what was going on next so much easier to deal with. Telling them he loved them as well, he put on his game face and was ready for whatever came next. Or so he hoped.

The semi drove by them about five minutes later. There were two men in the front of the cab; one of them was working for them, the other the driver that had been assigned to do the job. He too was singing about how many times he'd been out here, what he knew about the loads, as well as the money he'd been making. No one had had to threaten the man, he just started talking the moment they asked him for his paperwork.

The cargo was met by the governor. He had a woman on

each arm, his swimsuit showing off his saggy old body. The drone that the Feds were using was getting in close enough to not only see that it was indeed him, but that he was the one signing the paperwork on it. As soon as the lock was opened, everyone moved in when Garth gave the order to hit the rest of the places.

The men were staying back, waiting for him to go in and arrest the governor. He was with Agent Garth, but he stayed back as he touched the man on the shoulder. When he turned to look at him, Paddy smiled, then he told him who he was.

"Patrick Garrett. I thought you were dead. Or you were supposed to be." Paddy told him he was here to place him under arrest. "No, I don't think so. You're not even in the right place, young man. You can't be doing this anyway. I'm innocent of you being shot."

"I'm here to arrest you for stolen goods." He looked at the container that he'd just unlocked and back at Paddy. "Why don't you show us all what you have in there, sir? And make sure that you smile for the camera. They have it all."

The governor started screaming about private property. Then that he had no idea what was in the truck, just that he thought it was his new furniture. Paddy pointed to the set of keys the governor had been handed that were obviously car keys, and he tossed them away from it, like that was going to help. When Agent Garth started to read him his rights, the man went berserk, saying that he was a twin of the governor, that it was entrapment. Every word that he said was being recorded on the drone that was over their heads. When the threats turned nasty, Agent Garth had him taken away and put into a waiting car.

The cops from his precinct were rounded up as well. Some

tried to escape by running into the woods, but the agents there were ready for them. It was better than he could have hoped for, this bust, and much more fun for him than he'd thought it would be.

The agents descended on the party like a pack of wolves. Food was tested, the liquor was confiscated. The county that they were in was a dry one, and it was against the law for anyone to bring it in. In addition to the liquor, there were enough drugs, pills, pot, and even some drugs in the drinks that had some of the men shaking their heads. The cars were also tagged and put in another container to take to the lab to be tested. There was talk that drugs were more than likely hidden in the cars.

The women that were in with the cars were looked over by the EMTs. Two of them had died on the trip over, and one was critical. She was rushed to the hospital, but died on the way there. It was a bad day for the governor of Ohio. Now he had murder charges on his docket. They walked over to the cruiser he was in and allowed him out to stretch his legs. Agent Garth told him what had happened so far.

"I want to call my attorney." Agent Garth told him he could do that when he was charged. "No, you can't charge me. I have something you can use. The police station. I was setting them up for the fall here. They were going to come here and get the goods, and I was going to have them arrested." He looked at Paddy.

"Don't look at me. You nearly had me killed because I was in your way."

The governor lunged at him, knocking him on his ass. Paddy stayed where he was. Assault was added to the list too.

"You mother fucker. Why didn't you just stay dead like we

hoped? Do you have any idea what kind of money it's going to take to clean this up?" He seemed to have just realized that he was being recorded, even though someone had told him several times. "I'm not saying another word. Only that I think you set this up to make me look bad. I will not be humiliated like this any longer. I'm going into my house, and I want you all off my property now."

He, of course, never made it to his house, but was taken back to the car. Agent Garth told Paddy that he'd done a good job. While they were tagging everything there and getting statements from the guests, he was taken aside.

"There was a shootout at the station. Four dead, two more wounded who look like they might not make it either. They opened fire about the time my men entered." Paddy asked if any of his men were hurt. "One wounded, but he'll be fine once he has a chance to shift. Captain Walton is one of the deceased. It looks like a self-inflicted gunshot to his head. You said that he warned you about what was coming to you that day, correct?"

"Yes. I'm not sure that whatever was going on he was really a part of it, but playing along. I have information that he never touched the money that he was given as kickbacks." Agent Garth told him he'd heard that too. "His kid, she's hurting badly. This is going to make her getting ahead nearly impossible."

"She'll be fine. And if anyone asks, you say 'what money?'" Paddy said he could do that. "Good. Also, it's going to be in my report that Captain Walton helped you with information there. There is a man there, he's talking, but he is a friend of a friend and doesn't want any part of this. He's a vampire you might know as well."

104

"Scott Huff." Garth nodded. "All right. I like this way better. What is Scott getting out of this? Surely something."

"Nope, and that's the way he wants it too. Quincey said that he'd make sure he got something from it. And not bad. He helped a great deal with this, and made sure you were safe too. Are you coming back here? To work?" In that moment, he decided and shook his head. "Too bad. They're going to need a new captain, crew, and men that can be trusted."

"I have a family I need to take care of. My sister is living with me now, and I find that I like it." Garth put out his hand and Paddy took it. "Thank you. For everything. You have no idea how much this was weighing me down."

"Ah, but I do. And thank you for your help too. Like I said, we've been trying to get this man and the station house for some time now. We just didn't know about the drugs or the cars. You did good. And so did the people helping you."

It was well after midnight when he left the estate. It would be taken too, along with the houses they'd found paperwork for in the offices. Along with a list of banks his money had been stashed in, there was a list of people that he had dirt on. Things were not going to go well for anyone in the higher offices here, not for a long time.

He was dropped off at the hotel he was staying at around one-thirty in the morning. His body was beat, and his mind was too numb to think about anything but sleep. As soon as he went into his room, he stood there for several seconds, just looking around. Smiling, he went to the first vase of flowers and read the card.

"Congratulations! I knew you'd come out a winner. Love you and miss you, Jake, Forrest, and Jenna." There were other cards with flowers too. A large box of chocolates from

105

his sister. A ham, of all things, from the governor of West Virginia. There was a large basket of fruit from Agent Garth, and it was signed "Great job."

Taking an apple from the basket, he was making his way to the bathroom to shower the day off him when he saw Henry. He was laying on the bed, asleep, in a pair of the ugliest pajamas he'd ever laid eyes on.

Taking his shower quickly and quietly, he got into bed with Henry. He turned to Paddy, kissed him on the mouth, and asked if he was all right.

"I am now. Thank you for this." He said it was his pleasure and rolled to his back. "Just hold me, please? I'm whipped, and I can hardly think beyond how tired I am."

"And that is my pleasure as well. Good night, Paddy. I'll see you in the morning." He held him until he was asleep. Paddy wanted to ask him when he'd gotten there and where Christy was, but his mind just shut down. He'd ask him tomorrow, he thought, before going down for the last time. Tomorrow things would look a lot brighter.

~~~

Devon read about the shakeup at the police station and the governor's mansion over his morning breakfast. Things were going badly for that town, he thought with laugh. In a few days he was going to read about his family dying in a horrific accident. Having money could make all kinds of things go your way, he thought with a grin. Maybe he'd run for the seat. Having lots of money to grease palms should certainly put him there.

Dinner last night had been spectacular. He'd had the finest cut of steak that he'd ever eaten. And since he'd not ordered anything else to go with it, he was able to eat a second

106

meal too. He was so glad that he'd picked this hotel to stay in. Being their one-millionth guest had paid off well for him.

Just as he was finishing up his breakfast, his cell phone rang. It wasn't a number he knew so he didn't bother with it.

Devon had gotten him a nice suit, two of them as a matter of fact, with his windfall from the vampire, Tom. Devon had bought a condo too, one that he had been able to pay cash for when he'd decided that he'd have to be close for things to start happening here. He was moving into it in a few days. Right now he was having the walls painted and new carpets put in right now. Then today he was going furniture shopping. It was a hell of way to end his dip into poverty.

He'd gotten two more bags of cash yesterday. Devon didn't even bother opening them. He had seven such bags now, each of them with more money than he could spend in a lifetime, he thought. But he was making a good showing of trying to make that happen.

His phone rang again, same number, and he ignored it.

Wondering briefly if he should continue with the plan for getting the money from his half-brother, he decided that he could never have too much of it. The vampire that he had getting it for him, he might just meet the sun, or someone would shoot him with silver. A lot of things could happen, and he didn't want to ever be without again.

Leaving the restaurant, he didn't bother with a tip. He'd rarely had the money to do so before now, and he wasn't going to just be laying money around for someone too stupid to get out and do what he'd done. Find a way to be rich.

Taking a cab to the first furniture store on his list, he was happy to be able to get all new things. Even his underwear was new, having bought it at the same shop he'd gotten his suits from. He nearly balked at the idea of paying forty dollars for one pair, but the moment he put them on, he knew that was what he wanted. Ordering ten more pair in different colors, he felt like a new man.

The furniture store was busy, but he didn't mind. Going to the living room department, he sat on several of the softest couches that he could see. Not even bothering with the prices on things, he simply picked out the set he wanted and gave the address where he wanted it to be taken. This was more fun than he'd had in a long time. And not having a care what things cost was liberating, he realized.

Within several hours he not only had his home furnished, but he'd also had picked out patterns for his plates and gotten a nice set of pots and pans that he wasn't planning on ever using. Not unless he hired himself a cook. Which wasn't a bad idea now that the thought had entered his head. Then he went to the linen area. This was going to be his most difficult place to buy from, he realized, when he saw what that entailed.

Devon knew nothing of linen. He knew soft when he felt it, but not what kind of towels he wanted. What needed to be used in the kitchen, or what sort of things he'd need to make a bathroom homey. Not that he cared for the term homey, but he didn't want to be sickened every time he entered the single room.

There were sets of things for every room, but what did he want them to say? Some of them were all the colors of the rainbow, which he thought too much. There were ones with fish on them, as well as elephants. Why someone would have a décor of elephants in a room where they took a shit was beyond him.

Devon was looking at the elegant white set when someone

came up behind him.

"You should really learn to answer your phone." He didn't know the man, so turned his back on him. "You should drop the idea that you have now, Devon, before someone, you namely, gets hurt. And you will, have no doubt about that."

"I have no knowledge what you might be referring to. Now if you don't mind, I'm doing some serious shopping, and you're bothering me." The man laughed, and he turned to look at him. "What is it you think you know? Nothing. Is this about the Winslow estate? If it is, then you should know that I'm the bastard son of a very important man, and I should have a part in the estate. It's my due."

"Like the money you're spending now is your due? By the way, there won't be any more of that coming your way. Victor has paid for his part in this." He asked who that was. "I believe you knew him as Tom. Tom is dead. He died a very violent and messy death too. Would you like to see it?"

"No."

Before he could move away, the man touched his head. And he saw it all, the way Tom had been not just killed, but tortured as well. His skin was peeled from his body, his fingers taken off one at a time with a pair of very sharp trimmers. Each wound was in vivid color, the blood splatter everywhere. And when his head was removed, the body just disappeared.

But it was too much for him, and Devon leaned over and puked up everything he had on his belly. Still the images came to him. The cleanup, the way Tom's clothing had been burned. When he sat down on the floor, Devon realized that he was alone...not even a sales person was nearby that he could call for help from. Just the man that had come to torture him. And he looked down at him with a very unfriendly smile.

"Leave this alone with the Winslow estate, or worse will happen to you."

He looked up at the man, making sure that he knew every inch of him. Every hair, scar, and shape of the man was burned into his memory. Because soon, very soon, Devon was going to kill him. But before he could gather himself up, the man changed.

The monster, no other word to describe him, grew before his eyes. His eyes darkened to resemble blood filled orbs. Teeth, long and sharp, stretched out over his lower lip and darkened as well. Blood…he knew it was blood that was there. And when he leaned toward him, Devon screamed, fought with him to try and keep him from touching him.

"Mr. Winslow?" He punched out at the voice and heard a scream. It took him several moments, terrifying moments, before he realized what he'd done. "Are you all right?"

He'd hit the saleswoman and knocked her down. She laid there, her mouth bloodied from his fist. The two men standing with him, over him, gave him a second or two of terror, but it wasn't that man, the one that had tried to eat him.

"Did you see him?" The men asked him who as they looked around. "That monster. He was here. Threatening me. I lashed out when she came at me. I thought it was him again. He was going to eat me."

"I'm sorry, Mr. Winslow. But when you started screaming, we came running over. There was no one here but you. You seemed to be having a bad dream. Could you have fallen asleep for a few moments and dreamt it?" He glared at the man. "Or not. I don't know. You were alone the entire time."

"I tell you there was a vampire here." Now they got up

110

and backed away from him. It was enough to make him see red. Then he looked at the men, and right behind them was the man again, blowing him kisses. "Right there. Behind you. He's right there, and he's a vampire."

Both men turned and had to have seen the man. He was so close to them that Devon was sure they were playing a joke on him. But it wasn't funny. None of it was. Standing up, not even bothering with the woman he'd hit by telling her he was sorry, he left the store. They'd deliver his things or not, but he was getting out of the place.

It took him all day to get over the feeling of the man lurking about every corner. Twice he was sure he saw him in store windows. And then when he was checking into his hotel room. Things were getting very strange, and he knew that it had to be those other Winslows that were doing it. They were trying to scare him off.

"It's not going to work. I'm made of sterner stuff." He almost said that he was made of Winslow stock, but right now he didn't care to be associated with those people. Not that he wasn't going to enjoy taking every penny they had, but he wasn't going to be made to look the fool.

Devon often wondered who his father was. His mother had been a whore, he knew that. And he was only a byproduct of her ways. It had been a sad day when he realized that not only was he not a real Winslow, but that his mother hadn't a clue who his father might have been. She told him that it could have been one of many men that were putting food in his belly and a roof over his head. Then when she'd gotten too old to service men, what he had called it when she had men over, their food and roof soon disappeared. Devon had hated his mom before that, but he wanted her dead after he found out that she wasn't going to be able to care for him at all.

"Stupid cunt. You'd think that she'd lay a little aside each night to keep me in stuff. But no, she had to pay bills and make sure that the cable was on." He had been the one that wanted the cable. But he'd only wanted it to drown out the sounds going on in the other room. "Fucking idiot. Why didn't she just sue Winslow for some extra cash?"

He had a lot of unanswered questions about that time in his life. Why, if his mom was only a whore, did Winslow even bother with her? Then there was the fact that he'd not pay her for her services. Mom had told him he was a freebie.

What the fuck did that mean? Freebie? Like he got a special pass because he roughed her up a bit when he fucked her? He never brought her shit either, like some of her men did...pretty flowers or some candy. He'd loved the candy and shit. But not good old Winslow. He'd come in, strip down, fuck his mom, beat the shit out of her, maybe even him if he was close enough, then leave. For that alone he should have all the money from the will.

And he would. Devon wanted every penny of the estate of Jacob Winslow. He wasn't dead, but he might as well be. He was set to go to trial soon for not just the death of his own mother, but also a few other things that Devon could no longer remember. Jacob was going to prison for a long time.

"It's mine. All mine." He was feeling a lot better once he was locked in his room. The television was on, playing loudly just to annoy the people in the next room. And he had dinner being served to him in an hour. Closing his eyes, Devon let his mind go over the events of the day, and realized that everyone was doing this to him. They had seen the man, and were in on it with the Winslow man. He was going to enjoy killing this guy and his sister.

"Damn it." He'd have to find himself someone to kill them. He'd forgotten that Tom, or Victor, or whatever his name was, wouldn't be able to. Being dead like he was sure did put a damper on what Devon had wanted. "It's like that all the time. Shit keeps happening to me to mess up my timeline on things."

He'd get it done, but not as soon as he'd hoped. It was a good thing he had his stash of money. Devon wouldn't know what to do without that. Letting sleep take him under, Devon already felt like he was getting shit done. He'd be so rich, he'd pay people just to tell him the time.

Chapter 8

Henry waited until the couple in front of him was done arguing. Sometimes when couples were killed at the same time, he would have to wait on the blaming game. It was what he called it when they blamed each other for their demise. Christy entered the room and whistled. It was quite impressive, and had the desired effect. They both shut up.

"He's trying to help you, and you're giving me a head pain." She grinned at him. "You should buy you one of those hammer things that the judge uses. That should work."

"You mean to get their attention?" She said to hit them with. "I like that plan. Yes, I really do. I'll put that on my list."

"You'd hit us? We're already dead, why would you hit us?" Christy sat down at the table he was working from. His notes were spread out about the couple that had been arguing. "We just want some help."

"Then do so without the bickering. Yes, you're dead, but I can't help you if you don't tell me what you want. And you've been made aware of the rules, so don't ask me to tell your kids you're still hanging around. I can't do that." The woman, Ruby, asked why not. "It's against the rules. You cannot have contact with the living for any reason. Especially not your own family."

"Are there a lot of rules?" He told Christy that there were hundreds, but mostly he only used a few of them. "Like what? Can you send them away without helping?"

"I suppose, but I'd never do that." Wally came in the room with them, and told him that he'd found what he had asked for. Reading it over, he looked at Ruby and Jess. "You weren't killed by either of you. It says here that you both were killed by one of the tram drivers in the city you were in when it lost control. And before you ask me, the thing is still under investigation and there are pending lawsuits."

"Can you tell our children to sue?" He said that he couldn't. "What good are you anyway? I want my kids to know we're here for them. Nope, you can't do that. I'd like for them to have money for our deaths, you can't do that. What good are you?"

"I get you answers, which I have. You know now that you weren't killed by each other. I don't know why it matters. You are both dead, but I helped you." He stood up and stretched his neck. "Now, if there is nothing else you want from me, anything that I can do for you, then I think our time here is finished."

They disappeared. He could do that too, send them away. Wally told him once when he asked that they went to their place of death. Or sometimes, if they were nice enough people and understood what they could and couldn't do, they went to their place of living. He didn't really care for the people, so he hoped they didn't go home.

The next man that came for his help was a younger man, dressed in a business suit with blood on his tie. He never mentioned anything that seemed out of order with the people that came to see him. So when he told him who he was, Wally went to find out what he could. But Christy was there for him on this man.

"I read about you. Not all of it. The words were too hard." Henry asked her what she'd read. "He killed his wife and her boyfriend. I didn't know you could have both."

"Normally you can't, but I can't say for a lot of people." She nodded and got up. While she walked around him, he watched her but didn't move. "Christy, if you're going to engage with the dead, you need to learn the rules."

"Wally told me some of them. I had a little boy come to see me. He was heartbroken. I helped him." Henry looked at Wally, who said she'd done a good job. "This man is a nice man. He only hurt his pretty wife because she was stepping out. I don't know what that meant, so I asked Paddy Cake."

"And what did he tell you?" She explained to him like he was sure that Paddy had told her. "I see. And Trevor here, you think he's a nice man? Why is that?"

"He worked really hard to give her what she needed, I think." Trevor nodded and said that he'd worked a lot of overtime for the things she wanted. "Yes. That was nice of you. Some people just don't care for you no matter what you do for them, huh?"

"No. They don't. I just have a single request. It's not really a request, but a question. Can you find out if the man she was having the affair with had a family? I didn't think of that when I was angry." Wally said he'd look and disappeared. Henry picked up the newspaper that he'd been reading over today. He thought it mentioned this murder. By the time he'd found the answer, Wally had returned.

"He was a single man. But he had a lot of women on the hook." Wally looked at Christy and told her he'd explain that later. "Not a nice man. He did this a lot then when things got to be too clingy from his mistresses; he'd let the hubby know and end it that way. You were early coming home, I guess. He only just started the affair with her a few weeks ago. They usually last a couple of months."

Trevor thanked them and then turned to Christy. "Learn the rules, please. I'm sure, like what you did to help the little boy, there are more children out there that would rather talk to someone like you." She asked him if he meant because she was retarded. "No, I didn't.... No. I meant kind and loving. You have a good heart, that's all I meant. And you're not retarded, Christy. You're a wonderful human being. Don't let anyone tell you anything else."

Henry saw a few more of the dead. Seeing them at a certain time helped him have a life outside of talking to ghosts. Just as he was ready to end it for this morning another man showed up, and he had been dealt with violently. He wasn't sure that Christy should be there, but she got up and left the room before he could ask her to.

"I want you to avenge my death." Henry told him he couldn't do that. "Sure you can. I even know who did this to me. I want them right here with me, so I can hurt them too."

"You can't hurt someone that is dead as well. And you can't ask me to avenge your death either. You were made aware of the rules when you passed on." The man, he said his name was Redd, told Henry that he was going to do it for him or else. "And what is it you think you can do to me, Redd?

You can't touch me or anyone else associated with or related to me. And believe it or not, I'm not the least bit afraid of you. I have powers too. You know that."

"You can't just leave a man hanging like this. He was only supposed to kill me off, so my wife could have the insurance money. But he messed me up. She couldn't even see me in the casket or nothing." Henry asked him if he knew that was against the law. "Sure I do. That's why I hired her brother to kill me off. I was dying anyway. I got me the cancer, and I didn't think it would matter much if I died now with a little help. And she could use the money. But he messed me up instead of just killing me off."

Shaking his head, Henry told him he couldn't help him. He'd just have to wait on his brother-in-law. When he said he wasn't sick, Henry told him it was time to go. Before Redd was gone, he touched the man to get more information on the murder. Sometimes he could help the police solve crimes with just a little more information than they had to begin with. Going to the kitchen, he found Paddy going over the file that had been delivered to him that morning.

"Do you think that Jake or Forrest would be able to look this over for me?" He said they'd do it. "I'm not sure what I'm reading here. It's a little over my head with the party of the first and shit like that." Christy told him he owed a dollar to the cuss jar. When he got up to put the money in the jar, Henry glanced at the paper.

"It's a contract. About money." He said that's what he'd gotten too, but he was not sure who he owed it to. "I'm not sure either. I had an attorney go over everything I got; it's too confusing."

After making the call, both Jake and Forrest showed up,

bringing Jenna with them. They'd been to the doctor and were out anyway. As their cook made things for them to snack on—to Henry it looked like a full meal—Jake went over the contract.

"Who do I owe? I tried to decipher that out, but all I got was a headache." Jake told him he didn't owe anyone. "Well, that's good. I was wondering how we'd be able to buy a house if we had to shell out that kind of money."

"You want to buy this one?" Henry said they thought it was out of their price range. "I doubt it. I'll cut you the family deal. We don't either one need the money, but we hate paying taxes on it. I really was going to sell it, and this will be perfect. You guys would be close."

"First, why am I getting this contract?" They all laughed, and Henry tried to think what this house would be worth on the open market. They did love this place with all the space, and it was so close to Jake and Forrest, as Jake had said. "I got it by registered mail this morning, and I've been working on it since."

"You don't owe anyone; the states of Ohio and West Virginia are paying you. But with the stipulation that you don't tell anyone what happened, how you came to know what was going on, as well as who might have been involved. There's a name here, Agent Garth. He's the one that recommended you for this, saying that you saved the state as well as the Bureau a great deal of money by coming to them with this issue." Jake pointed out that they knew about it. "Yes, it does mention that as well, but it says too that there isn't any timeline where they were going to finish their investigation up within the next five years or so. That's what they're saying anyway."

"So, let me get this straight. Because I got shot at and my

ass was on the line, I did some digging with the help of a lot of people, and they're going to pay me to keep my mouth shut? Okay. I don't know who I'd talk to about it anyway, but sure." Paddy looked at Henry. "Whatever it is, we'll go out and celebrate or something. I don't know."

"You can do that and more. They're giving you what it would have cost them in working hours, overtime as well as any other costs, such as court and man power, to have a trial. It says here that the acting governor has written out a statement saying that you were instrumental in all that went down, including at the station house where you worked." Jake grinned. "You are being awarded just over six million dollars. And the check is already at the bank where you've opened an account, waiting for you to come in and sign this contract in front of the bank manager."

"No way." Jake nodded. "Are you serious? That's a shit load of money. There has to be some kind of mistake."

"I doubt they'd own up to it if it was a mistake, but it's legal. If you want to go to the bank now, we can finalize that part and sell the house to you. Forrest and I were going to talk to you about it soon anyway, and we're happy to have you here." He named an ungodly low price. "I've told you this before, but this house had some bad memories in it for us. But since you've been living here, I can come here and not think about my grandma being gone, nor that my father nearly killed me. The house is yours if you want it. And it includes all the furnishings. We already took out what we wanted when we moved."

"Yes, we'll take it." Henry looked at Paddy when he spoke, laughing. "That is, if Henry wants to. I should have talked it over with you first. Sorry. I just love this place."

"Me too. And yes, I agree, we'll take it. But, there are a couple of things I want too. First of all, you two will consider this your home too. I know you're not far from us, but come over anytime you want and visit us. The second one is easier. If you agree, I'd like to see if you have a guardian for Jenna, and if you don't, would you consider us?"

"Deal and deal." They all hugged after shaking hands. They were homeowners together. It was a big step, Henry knew that, but it didn't scare him. It felt right, like this was just the right thing to do right now. Sitting down and listening to them talk, Henry didn't think he'd had better friends his whole life.

He was handed Jenna as plans were made to go to the bank. She was such a little beauty. Her light hair made her look like she was hairless there, but if you looked closely enough, you could see it. Her eyes were blue, but he knew that as she grew older, they might change as well. But Jake's were blue too, and he'd bet anything that Jenna would keep hers as he had. When she pursed her little lips, he had to smile. She was already learning how to wrap someone around her little tiny fingers.

As they got ready to go, he thought of the sale of his house back home. He should put it on the market, sell it, and perhaps buy more property here. It was a good investment, and he and Paddy would need something to do. He wasn't bored yet, being jobless, but he knew it would hit him soon enough. Time to get his butt in gear.

~~~

Paddy had never had money. Not even when he wasn't paying for his sister's care. He'd been making his payments, but that was about it. Not much in the way of entertainment,

122

and certainly no money for a house. Now he had both. But he wasn't going to be stupid with it. While at the bank with Jake, he asked him to set up a trust fund for his sister.

"I can do that for you. It's actually a very good idea. The house will be in both yours and Henry's name, I'm assuming." He told him that they'd not even discussed it. Paddy turned to Henry, who was laughing. "What?"

"What's mine is yours, Paddy. And I think that having a trust fund for Christy is a great idea. She should also have an account, so she can spend her own money. I'm going to hire her too, to help me with my projects." Paddy knew that she'd been helping Henry out, but he hadn't known that the ghosts were coming to see her alone too. He was all right with that, but it still worried him a little. "The pack is showing her how to use a computer too. As well as having her read to the younger children. She's making quite the name for herself there, as well as in town."

"She's not causing trouble, is she?" Henry told him that she'd been at the library helping with the books. As well as the local grocery store wanted to hire her to help bag groceries. "She said that she was having fun. I guess after being cooped up in that place for so long, she's enjoying her freedom."

He opened her a checking account and put money in it for her. She would have to come in and set up her account with her signature, as well as her pin for the card, but he felt better about it. Paddy would have to talk to her about spending, and how to keep a tight grip on the card. He didn't want her hurt or ripped off.

It took them two hours to get everything squared away. Paddy called his sister and asked if she wanted to have dinner with them in town. When she said that she would and that she was close to them, he was happy to tell her to come to the bank and finish up the paperwork. Christy squealed and told him she'd be right there.

Her handwriting was getting better, he noted. And she was dressed in a very pretty dress with sandals. Paddy could only stare at her. He'd not realized that she was a full-grown woman. When Forrest laughed, he looked at him and told him what he was thinking.

"I know, it's written all over your face. But you'll be happy to know that, not only is the pack watching out for her, but the streak that I'm in is as well. No one will live that touches her." He thanked him. "No need for that. I had the same awareness the other day. She has such a child-like quality to her that you forget that she's in her early twenties."

Yeah, Paddy forgot that as well. Then he pulled out his phone and realized that her birthday was in a few days. He wanted to have her a party. Not a huge one, but one where she had friends over, gifts, and a cake. If she wanted one. Taking her aside while they waited on their table at the restaurant, he asked her what she wanted for her birthday, and she hugged him.

"You've given me so much. I don't need anything at all." He told her surely she wanted something. "Nope. But maybe you could take me shopping. I don't have many pretty things to wear. When I was trapped, I had to wear jammies. I'm sick of them."

"All right. Shopping it is. Do you want a party? Or a nice dinner out with friends." She told him she'd think about it, and he laughed. "I bet you have a lot of friends now, don't you?"

"I do. And I have a job if you'll let me take it." He asked

her what sort of job, not wanting her to know that he'd already heard that she was looking. Then she told him about the grocery store that had asked her to come in two days a week, and that she liked working at the library. "They said that since I know my ABC's I can help sort the books into bins for them. I won't be paid, but that's all right with me. I like helping the people that come in."

"I'm very proud of you, honey. You've come a long way, haven't you?" She said she felt good about herself, and Doris, the pack leader's wife, had told her that was good too. Christy looked up at him with a sad face. "What is it? Is someone bothering you? At the library or the pack?"

"No. I was wondering if, now that you have Henry and all, you'd send me back to that place. I don't want to go, but if you don't want me around anymore, I can pay for myself." He hugged her to him, overwhelmed with an emotion that he couldn't name. "I love you, Paddy Cake, but I'd understand."

"Neither one of us wants you to go anywhere." He asked Henry to come over and told him what she'd said. "She thinks that now that we have each other, she won't be as welcome."

"Oh honey, that could never be true. Ever. You own my heart as much as you do your brother's. I love you, and would never want you to go away, not even if you had three jobs."

When Jake and Forrest overheard what they were saying, they told her that she was going to babysit for them when Jenna got a little older. Christy asked if she'd get paid, and everyone laughed. It was a good time, having everyone together, and Paddy was glad more and more every day that he'd been found by these people and brought into their lives.

When they were on their way home, Henry stopped walking. He asked him if he was all right when he turned and looked where he was pointing. There, standing in the doorway to one of the empty buildings on the main street, was a small person. From where he was standing, Paddy couldn't tell it if was male or female. Before he could decide what they needed to do, his sister walked over and got down on her knees with the child.

After a few minutes, she waved them both over. The closer they got to them, he could see that the little boy, he could see now, had been hurt. And badly. The entire left side of his head was crushed in, and his arm hung limply at his side. Christy was explaining to them, at least Henry, what was going on when Paddy knelt down as well.

"Where are they?" The young boy looked at Christy, then back at him. "I'm her brother. But you look like you've only just been hurt. I'm assuming that there are others with you. Are any of them alive?"

"I don't know, but I think my mom is. Am I dead? I think I am, but I don't know." Not sure what to tell him, he asked him if he could take him to the accident. Because Paddy had seen enough injuries like this child had to know that it was a bad one. "We was coming home from Grandma's, and I heard a loud popping sound."

Paddy walked with him as the little boy explained what he thought had happened. It sounded like a tire blow-out, but without seeing it, he wasn't sure. As they came upon the accident, not far from town, he told Henry to call an ambulance as well as the police. Nodding, he did so without question. Paddy asked the little boy what his name was.

"I'm Howard James Lucas. But my momma, she calls me Bugger. Can you help her? My dad is there too, but I'm not worried about him. Grandma said only the good die young,

126

and he ain't good."

Paddy told him he was sorry and moved to the overturned vehicle. He could see inside the front window, and knew that the dad was dead...his neck was broken. Going to the mom, he felt her pulse and knew while it was there, it was very weak. She opened her eyes and looked at him.

"I'm going to get help. Is there anyone else in the car besides you and your husband?" She said that her son was in the back. "I'll see to him."

Paddy didn't tell her Bugger was already gone; he didn't want her to give up or to get hysterical. Asking her again about anyone else, she shook her head. He could hear the sirens as they made their way to them, and Paddy asked Henry to guide them to him.

In twenty minutes they had extricated the father and mother. She died from her wounds a few minutes later. The husband was dead when they arrived, he told the police. Giving them the report that he'd been out walking with his family when he saw the smoke, they seemed to believe him. Henry and Christy backed up his story. Paddy wasn't sure what they'd say if he told them that the dead son had led them there.

Giving them his phone number and address, they seemed to know the house well. Asked about Jake and Forrest, they talked about the pretty little baby that they were raising. Since he didn't have any idea what the town thought of the two of them, all he said was that Jake had sold the house to them. His sister needed space to live in.

"I've seen her around town, your sister. She's a pretty little thing, isn't she? Nobody will bother her, Mr. Garrett. We've all got someone in our family that is little different.

She's a little too trusting, and just has a heart of gold someone will hurt. You don't have to worry none about her, we watch her like she's our own." He thanked him. "You're welcome. To tell you the truth, my little boy, Will, he can't talk about anything else but how she comes in and helps him in the library. My wife, she just thinks the world of her too. She working at the grocery now?"

"She is. Christy, her name is Christy, she is going to be working there a few days a week." He nodded and looked over at Henry. He was almost afraid of what was going to spew from his mouth.

"That your partner too, I'm assuming. He's a nice man. Helped me the other day when I had some trouble at home. Good men, both of you are. I'm glad that you've decided to come stay in our little town." Paddy thanked him. "Like I said, we all have someone in our family that isn't like everyone else, but it matters little to us so long as you're a good person. And you both are."

When he walked away, Paddy felt like he'd been given a new outlook on life. No one had ever been so kind to him, not ever, when they found out what he was, a gay man with a lover. And for them to be so accepting of his sister made him want to shout from the rooftops that he'd found a home. Yes, he thought, he was going to be very happy here.

Chapter 9

Devon sat on the floor in his new place. His furniture had been delivered just today, but he was sitting on the floor instead of enjoying the softness of it against his back. The linens that he'd bought were still in the plastic bags; not even the wash cloths he'd gotten to go with them were used. It would all have to go back, or be repossessed, if this thing with the Winslows didn't get finished soon. And he wasn't going to be charged for them being mussed up. Even though the condo was paid for, there would still be taxes and utilities that he wasn't sure right now how he was going to pay for. Nothing, it seemed, was going his way.

Finding someone to kill his brother and sister was becoming a problem. He'd contacted two men that he'd found on the Internet, of all places, and they wanted upfront money first. Like he had it. Devon looked over at the several money bags that he'd opened today. They were all filled with fake money. All wrapped up in nice neat packs like you'd get from the bank, but it wasn't money he could use. Unless someone had elected a duck as someone to put on money, he was screwed.

All he wanted to do was cash in on the money that belonged to him. Laughing a little, he knew that it didn't actually belong to him, but it would if he could get someone to help him. He'd kill them himself, his brother and sister, but that would make him guilty of murder on top of everything else, and he wasn't sure he'd get off from that, no matter how much money he had when it was over.

Getting up from the floor, he sat down on the couch. He wasn't going to be in this self-pitying mood any longer. Devon decided right then that he had to do this. What other way did he expect to be a rich fuck if he didn't get his family murdered so he could get it all?

"A few months ago I might have taken half, but no more." Even as he said that, he knew it for the lie that it was. There wasn't any way he was only going to be half as wealthy as he wanted to be. His daddy had wanted him to have it, or he would have said something to the contrary.

The knock at his door startled him from his thoughts. Getting up, he looked in the peephole, but didn't know the man on the other side. Asking what he wanted only got him a mumbled response. Devon drew his gun and put it behind him as he opened the door. The man there was good looking, he supposed, with a big guy on campus look about him. Devon asked him what he wanted.

"Nice place you have here." He didn't bother telling him that was why he'd picked it. "You Devon Winslow? Self-proclaimed bastard son of Jacob Winslow?"

"I am. What's it to you?"

The envelope was shoved in his hand before he got the

chance to say any more. The man explained that he'd not have to sign anything, as they were recording things. When he was gone, walking to his car that was still running, Devon opened it to see what the hell was going on.

"What the holy fuck?"

He was being summoned to appear in court in a week, to settle the claim he was making against the Winslow estate, and one Jake Winslow, and Jenna Winslow. He hadn't known what the kid was called, but now he knew. And the fact that she'd not had to wait until she was eighteen to change her name made him think that someone had known for sure that it was a child of Jacob's.

Devon spent the rest of the afternoon trying to track down an attorney. He couldn't afford a retainer right now, and he was sure that once he won this thing, lawyers would be coming out of the walls to work for him. But right now, all he could get was a court appointed one, and that was the bottom of the barrel as far as he was concerned. But what else was he supposed to do? Go there and asked for some of his money now so he could sue them back? Devon didn't think that would go over well.

Once he had someone to talk to, he had to gather up all his paperwork on his claim. He had a copy of the doctored DNA test, as well as pictures of Jacob Winslow and his mom. In one of them she was holding a baby; she had claimed it wasn't him, but he had said it was. And since she was dead and couldn't tell differently, he kept the lie up.

Once the man came to his home, Lou Clay was his name, he spread it all out on his new table. He wanted to tell the man to use a coaster when he had a glass of tea, but decided that was going too far, even for him. Instead, he sat with him

131

at the table and asked if it was enough.

"They will more than likely ask you for a second DNA test." He said that he wasn't going to do that. "Why not? I mean, it's not like it could come back saying you're someone else's kid. And even if it does, you can always claim that it wasn't done right or something. That'll delay things, and people hate delays more than they do anything."

"How long of a delay will it be if I refuse? And I'm going to." He shrugged and said it could be a few months or several years. "I don't have several years. I want the money coming to me now. My father's estate should have been split with me. And that's why I want it all. They knew I was out there. And even if they didn't, it's well past time that they acknowledged me."

Devon liked the sound of that. They should acknowledge him in some way. When this was done, he would demand it. That they would have to take out an entire page in the local newspaper—hell, around the world—and say they'd been wrong, he was their half-brother.

After two hours, he had a list of things that could and more than likely would be brought up. Jacob Winslow's name wasn't on Devon's birth certificate. He'd not come to the hospital to see him being born, another tick against the man. And this was the really scary one, Devon was more than likely going to be ordered to take another test, if for no other reason than to get him to shut up about being a Winslow.

"It doesn't help that you changed your name to Winslow. I know you have proof that he was your father, but without a lot of other factors to prove you right, then they're going to win." Lou asked him if he still wanted to proceed with this. "If it can be proven that any of this evidence you have was paid for, that you had it faked or that you've been lying the entire time—I'm not saying you are, Mr. Winslow—but if they can prove even one of these are false, you might end up in prison with your dad."

"No. That can't happen. I'm just a man who would like to have someone say, here you go, I'm sorry that we put you through this." Lou asked him what they'd done. "Well, nothing. I mean, other than not to tell me I'm their brother and that I should have been a part of this entire thing."

"I don't know how much luck you're going to have getting your father's estate either, to be honest. He's in prison, not dead. And even if he were to die or have something happen to him, as his legal son, Jake would get his estate. You can petition for a part of it, but that's about all."

"Why are you so negative about all this? Shouldn't you have something good to say to me about this? I would think you would have to." He said that he was preparing him for the worst. "There is no worse than me having nothing."

"You have a nice home. Beautiful new furniture. You have a car, money in the bank, and you're wearing a very expensive suit. I don't think you can claim that you've been living without. No one will believe that." Damn it, Devon thought, he'd fucked up by buying him a home. "What I would suggest you do before the hearing is think about having another test done, one where there are witnesses as well as a notary. Have them sign all the paperwork with you, and keep a copy. That way, you can jump the gun on having it ready. I don't think you're going to have the results by the hearing, but you can show that you're willing to meet then halfway on this. Also, maybe you can go to the prison and talk to your father. Perhaps you can get him to sign off on you being his son. That'll help you a great deal."

See his father? He had to laugh a little bit there. Like who would he like to tag in that query? According to his mom, she was seeing dozens of men when she'd conceived him. It didn't help that even back then, there was nothing to prove that she was anything more than just a single woman with a son trying to make ends meet.

Devon had no choice in the matter now. He was going to go to this hearing as prepared as he could. And if that meant that he had to go up and see his supposed father, then that was what he'd do. Perhaps he'd tell him he'd share the money with him, which he wouldn't, if he would just do this one thing for him. It was the least he could do after fucking his mom for free all those years.

He hadn't any idea what would be required of him to visit someone in prison. The only experience he had with something like this was watching it on television. And he was sure that wasn't even close to being correct. Devon had his passport that he'd gotten recently when he had money, his driver's license, and then as an afterthought, he went to the store and picked up a few magazines as well as some candy bars. Again, this was only from watching programs, but he thought, who wouldn't like a little sweet treat once in a while? Devon nearly bought some cigarettes, but decided at the last minute not to do that. They were fucking expensive anyway. A carton of really cheap ones was anywhere from thirty to forty dollars, and the name brand ones were sixty to seventy bucks. Screw that shit.

Devon would start out first thing in the morning and make a day of it. It wasn't a long trip, about two hours, but he was going to have fun. And if daddy dearest wouldn't help him, he'd have to tell him a lie. And Devon was thinking about that too...what to tell a man who had nothing left to lose that would piss him off enough that he'd help him get back at his son.

"You have to have something."

Devon decided to take a walk. It was a lovely evening, and perhaps something would come to him. When he was about a five-minute walk from his home and near the grocery store, he saw the man that had served him. He was with another man and a woman. The woman entered the grocery, pulling on a smock like he'd seen them wearing in there. Wondering who they were, he nearly called out to the man when the two of them kissed.

Devon was revolted by it. He hated gays almost as much as he did shifters and the like. The men walked away, holding hands and greeting people just like they were a nice normal couple. Devon wanted to find a gun and shoot them both. Rid the world of their disgusting ideas.

Thinking that he was going to give them a piece of his mind by just walking up and telling them off, he saw a police officer pull over and get out of his cruiser. Devon was excited now. They'd be told to move on or leave. That they had no business around real people. But none of that happened.

"Hello, Forrest, Jake. I was wondering if you have a minute." Devon stood stock still. He'd just called that man Jake. As in Jake Winslow. He didn't wait around to find out what he wanted and made his way home instead. This was his half-brother. His homo, take it up the ass half-brother.

Devon wondered if his father knew...or for that matter, if anyone knew. He wasn't really related to the man, but now he was glad. For the first time since he'd started this thing, he was glad that he wasn't a real blood relative of the man kissing bastard. Shivering at the thought, he decided that he had enough information to go to Daddy now. And he wondered if he'd sign off on the paperwork now that he had a gay son.

"He'll be so glad to have a normal red-blooded American son that he'll do just about anything for me." Laughing and doing a little jig around his living room, Devon went to bed a happy man. Things were finally going his way.

~~~

"You have a visitor." Jacob looked up at the officer who had been on duty since six this morning. He knew this because it was the only way that he could tell that a day had passed. The fucking system couldn't even put him in a cell with a window. No, he had to be in maximum security because of what he'd done as a lawyer. "You want to see them or not? I can tell him to go."

"My son?" He hoped the Christ not. He had nothing to say to him. "If it's Jake, tell him I don't fucking have anything to say to him."

"No, not Jake. This guy is Devon Winslow. Any relation?" Jacob just shrugged. "You want to see this guy? He has some stuff for you, Jacob. Candy and some magazines."

"Yes, I'll see him."

He stood up, not knowing the drill for having a visitor. The only person he'd seen was a court appointed attorney, and he was as dumb as horse shit. He was told to back up to the bars, where he was cuffed from behind. Then when he turned around, his ankles were chained together with a short chain. Same way he'd left the cell when he saw the shit for brains.

136

Going down the long hallway, he thought about how far he'd fallen. A man of worth, or so the world thought. A man who was wealthy, also only in the eyes of the people around him. He hadn't had a job in longer than he'd actually worked. His mother, the fucking cunt, had made sure that his bills had been paid and that he had money in the bank, just so long as she could have Jake as much as she wanted.

Jacob had cut her off from Jake once. Telling her that not only was she a bad influence on him, but she was taking him places that would make him, as his father, look bad. The races, and to dining establishments that he'd not send his butler in. But she had cut him off as well. And for an entire week and a half, ten days, he'd lived in hell when his credit cards no longer worked, and he didn't have a limo to call on.

Minor things to some, but it was his life, and she had humiliated him in those ten days that he never forgave her for it. And now the old bitch was dead, and his son was taking over just where she had left off. Dirtying the name Winslow, like they had any right to. And he was in prison.

Sitting in the windowed off area, he wondered who this Devon person was. More than likely it was a fake name to get in and talk to him about what had happened that night. To him it had been a good thing and bad. His mother was gone, but he wasn't getting any of her money. And his wife was dead as well.

While waiting on the other person to come in, he thought of Trina. She had been a perfect match to him and his lifestyle. There had never been a cross word between them. He did what he wanted, she did what she wanted. The affairs that they both had were nothing serious, and he never claimed any of the bastards that were a product of them. To his way

137

of thinking, he was a Winslow, and did not wear condoms for low lifes. To him and his name, everyone was lower than him.

The young man that sat down looked familiar. He couldn't place him, but he was certain that he knew who he was. When he picked up the phone, Jacob did as well. And when he said his name, Jacob asked him what he wanted.

"I'm your son." He started to hang up but saw the kid shaking his head. Putting the phone back to his ear, he listened to him. "You and my mom had this long affair. She was Becky Shiner. We lived on Maple."

"Yeah, so? What do you want? In the event you might not have noticed when you came here, I'm in prison. If you're claiming to be my by-blow, then you're shit out of luck. I don't have my checkbook." The kid laughed, and just like that, he knew just who he was. "You're not my kid. Your mom was fat with you when I started coming around."

"I'm a Winslow. And if you help me out with this thing with your son, I'll give you some of the cash that I'm going to get from your estate." He asked him what estate. "Yours and your wife's. I should have a part of it. You screwed my mom for a lot of years, not paying her a dime and beating her around. I want...no, I deserve it. You help me out and I'll help you."

Jacob wondered if the idiot knew that they were being recorded. When he nodded like he was sure he was going to agree, Jacob decided to have some fun. When he was finished, he'd be back in his cell without anyone to talk to, and he figured that this would be some entertainment for him.

"They said that you brought some things for me." He nodded at the officer by his side, and a stack of magazines that he'd never read were laid in front of him. A bag of candy bars, all chocolate, as well as a large bag of pretzels. Nothing in it that he'd have anything to do with if he wasn't in here. "This is crap. What the hell am I supposed to do with this? There's enough sugar in just one of these bars to make a person sick for a week."

The officer on his side cleared his throat. He was getting loud again, something they frowned upon, apparently. Shoving the things to the side, knowing that he'd trash every bit of it when he got out of here, he asked him about the estate.

"Jake has it all. Did you know that he's gay? Christ, your wife must be rolling over in her grave right now. I saw them. The two of them holding hands and kissing. It about made me sick. You help me with this hearing I'm to have, and I'll set you up in style." He told him he wanted out. "Well, I don't know how to make that happen for you. But I can get you an attorney that'll be the best there is. I mean, with your estate coming to me, there isn't anything I couldn't do for you."

"You do know that I'm not dead, right? I mean, you can't inherit until I'm dead and cold in my grave." The kid told him that he had no use for it, not in here, and he'd keep it safe for him, if he got out. Jacob knew that he was never getting out of here. "I don't know how you think that's going to work. But hey, I'm just a convict."

He had hoped that the kid would say something like he'd been framed or that he didn't believe he'd done anything wrong. Killing his mom had gotten him a lot of grief here. He'd never known how far reaching her humanitarian work had been.

"This attorney I have, he said that if I could get you to claim that I'm your son, by an affair with my mom, then I can at least get a portion of what Jake has. I'm still not sure why they'd like a thing like him have anything that belonged to decent human beings, but I don't run the laws. Anyway, I can have you sign your name that claims that I'm your kid too, and that way he'll have to fork over a part of what he and his sister have."

"Sister? He doesn't have a sister." Devon told him that they had adopted another one of his bastards. "No, I'm not sure where you got your information, but I think someone would have mentioned me having another kid out there."

"I've not seen her, but I guess her mother died right after this kid was born. The gays took her, and the adoption was announced just yesterday morning. Her name is Jenna. Can you imagine what your poor mom thinks about that thing having a child named after her?" Jacob thought that his mother would have loved it, and would have rubbed it in his face every chance she got. "Anyway, she's yours. They had tests done. I think the paper said that it would be another nail in your coffin, or something like that. The newspapers can be so cruel when they want."

Jacob sort of half-listened to what the idiot was saying. A child? He wondered if after all this time it was even possible. He'd had a vasectomy right after Jake was born. Jacob wished every day after the death of his son that he'd never done that. Benny had been his perfect child. The one that played sports, won awards, and had good grades. When he was killed in an accident that should have been Jake instead of his Benny, it had nearly killed him and his wife to lose their favorite child like they had. And then to be stuck with such an imperfect creature as Jake had been. Also, to find out that he was gay, that was just too much.

The idiot was staring at him, as if he was waiting on him

to agree or answer. He just looked around and pretended to consider whatever he had said. But when he just stared, like he was stupid or something, he asked him what he wanted him to do.

"Just sign the paperwork. I can help you by you helping me." He pointed out again that he wasn't his son. "Yeah, you know that, and I know that, but they don't have to know, now do they? And this will make sure that I don't have to do any DNA testing. I'll fail that for sure."

Jacob didn't have any idea what to think of this kid. He was either really stupid, which was the way he was thinking, or he really thought that he was impervious to any kind of laws. When he had the paperwork handed to him, Jacob read it over.

At one time he'd studied law — well, he'd gone to college to study it — and had graduated with a degree. What he'd learned for the most part was how to have a good time. But those days were behind him as soon as he got out. Jacob became a respectable Winslow, much to the disappointment of his mother.

Mother had thought that everything was a joke of some kind, and that she was to have fun at life. She'd become an embarrassment to him and Trina, so much so that they considered having her committed. But that, too, had fallen through, and she'd cut him off again. After that, Jacob never bothered with her if he didn't have to, and ignored her as much as he could when she was in the paper for something that she'd done.

"It should be marked where you're supposed to sign it." Jacob thought that he should pay better attention to Devon. He might end up in the cell next to him, and he wasn't sure

141

that would go over well. After signing his name to every place that had a yellow tab had been put, he handed it back to the guard to give to Devon. When he was done, the kid seemed to want to take off.

"Wait. I don't have anyone to talk to for hours on end. Just...we have like ten more minutes. Just tell me about the weather." He looked at him strangely. "Look dumbass, I did what you wanted. Now the least you can do is talk to me about the weather. Is it raining? Snowing? I don't know, something."

"It's pretty out. A nice fall day. I had the windows down as I drove up here." Nodding, he asked him if the trees had turned yet. When he was out, he never cared a fig for the trees, just that the yard man would make a mess at the end of the driveway with them. Now, it was all he could think about. The weather, the restaurants that someone might go to. Anything that had nothing to do with prison.

When his time was up, Devon stood up. Jacob couldn't, not until he was released from the hook on the floor. As he sat there, waiting his turn to be taken back to his cell, he wondered if his wife didn't have the right idea. Killing himself would have been a good deal better than what he had in here.

Shuffling back to his cell, he nearly sobbed when he sat down. It felt like he had had a taste of freedom, or at least a small part of being a human again, and to return here was like a slap in the face. Sitting on the bed, he felt like a man on his last legs, and wondered if it could ever get any worse than it was right now.

Jacob didn't regret killing his mother. Had she just not tried to save his son, he would have eventually gotten around to having her knocked off as well. Or, she would have died of a broken heart. Either way would have been fine by him. Yes, he might have gone to prison for it, but he would have gotten off. Being introduced to your son's male lover would make anyone lose control. But when he'd killed his mom and there was no one there to back him up on how it had happened, he was the one made to suffer. And suffer he had.

Chapter 10

The courtroom was packed with people. Henry had met most of them while he was taking his daily walk around the town, but there were a lot of television crews there, as well as newspaper columnists. When someone said his name, he turned and waved. Henry wasn't going to hide anymore, and he was happy to have Paddy in his life.

Last night the family attorney had come to talk to them. He was a nice little man…a very good friend of the family too. He'd told them he was glad to still be of service to them, and sat down and told them what he wanted and what was, he hoped, going to happen.

"The young man went to see your father yesterday." Jake had been surprised by that, but Mr. Crenshaw told him that the recording had been printed and it would be helpful in the case. "Devon is about the dumbest crook I've ever run across. I kid you not. He told your father what he hoped would happen by having him sign a document that states he's his child. Which, Devon knows that he's not."

145

"Why would he do that? I mean, he did know he was being recorded, didn't he?" Mr. Crenshaw said he asked the same thing, and they told him that they tell them when they ask to see someone, and there is a sticker on the booth as well as the phone. "What did my father say about this?"

"He did it. I'm not sure of his reasoning, but he signed the paperwork. But the strangest thing, he also left a note for me to see his physician. Did you know that your father had a vasectomy a few days after you were born?" Jenna took that moment to fuss, and Mr. Crenshaw laughed. "I have it on good authority that those procedures from that long ago weren't as thorough as they are now. Miss Jenna is his child, no doubt about that. But there isn't any way that Devon is. Devon even admits to it."

"Then why do all this if he knows?" Mr. Crenshaw said he didn't know, but they would more than likely find out at the trial. And here they were, waiting on the judge to come out and get this started.

He watched the younger man. Devon looked nothing like Jake, but then he supposed that was possible as they had different mothers. The kid was cocky and dressed in a suit that Henry thought cost about four grand. His shoes were expensive as well, and he had to laugh every time he reached down to wipe at them. Like he was going to return them when this was over.

Henry thought about the things they'd had to do yesterday in order to make their home theirs. It wasn't anything terrible, but it had been exhausting. They'd gone through each of the bedrooms and decided what they wanted to do with them. It had been fun just making the place look like what they wanted.

For the most part each of the rooms were empty of furnishings. He had heard from Forrest that when Jake's ex-wife, Carol, had decided to teach Jake a lesson, she'd taken all the furniture and even the food from the house and put it into storage. Forrest said it was nothing that anyone in their right mind would want anyway, and they were glad it had been taken care of. And he thought that even a blind person would turn it down, it was that ugly. The walls, recently painted a plain white, had been just as loud as the furniture.

They had so much to work with, and they both knew that rushing into things would be problematic. Not that they didn't want to fill each of the rooms with their own things, but really, neither of them had that much. Henry had a house in California, but it had only been a small ranch with two bedrooms...one his, the other his mom's. And the kitchen had been remodeled last in the early fifties, and it looked it. The retro look was nice, out there. Here, it wouldn't have flown well.

When they were told to rise, and he did with everyone else.

"We're here to determine if Devon Winslow has a right to be claiming that he should have gotten a part of the estate of one Jenna Winslow, deceased." Devon corrected the judge. "What do you mean, you're only concerned about the estate of Jacob Winslow? Last I heard, he was still alive, much to the shame of this town."

"He's the heir to her estate, and that's what I should have a part of. I know that she's deceased and all, but I know that her son was to get it all. That's what I should have a share of. Not the elderly woman. She probably didn't have anything anyway. Women tend to spend willy nilly."

147

The courtroom burst out laughing, even the judge laughed. Telling Devon to sit down and shut up, he looked at his counsel and told him to keep his client quiet.

As he read the rest of today's hearing notes, Henry watched Jake. The man had been through a lot more than he'd realized. Not only had he been married to an irrational nut ball of a wife, but his family had basically sold him to her family. And if that wasn't enough, Carol had killed her own mother by beating her to death, and then told the police that she'd done her daddy a favor by killing her, she was a drag anyway. There was more too, so much more that he wondered how Jake was not a basket case, as Henry might have been. But then, Henry thought that being in love would do that for you.

Paddy and he had decided last night that they were going to travel a great deal now. The money that they'd gotten was going to set them up for a lot of things that would be good for the two of them as well. They had decided on getting a nice camper, so that when they traveled they'd not have to go to hotels, where they might not be as welcome as they were here.

When Jake was asked to stand and give his side of what had been going on, Henry listened to him. He was to make a few points, none of them mentioning the transcript from the jail. They'd do that, Mr. Crenshaw had told him, when the time was right.

"There have been several people, your honor, who will testify that Mr. Winslow, Devon, has asked them to have myself and my sister killed." Devon jumped up, but was pulled back to his seat by his attorney. "The day that my sister was born, he had a man there that was to snatch her from us and take her somewhere to be sold off, we believe, or simply murdered. Mr. Huff has sent a signed statement telling of the plan."

The courtroom began talking all and once, and turned to look at Devon. He stood up again, but no amount of pulling from his attorney would make him sit down.

"I can explain that. You see, they weren't answering my emails, nor would they see me. It was a scare tactic. It never meant anything." The judge must have had a copy of the statement from Scott. "Now that we're all here together, I think we can get this settled once and for all. Don't you think?"

"According to this, you told him to kill the child, and if he got the chance, he was to kill Jake as well. That you had something of his. A coin that he gave to people that he owed a favor to. And you stole that." The judge looked at Devon. "If I have to tell you again to sit down and shut up, I'm going to find you in contempt of court."

Jake continued on about how he'd not received any messages from Devon, and had he, Jake said that he'd have referred him to the family attorney. Devon wasn't standing now, but he wasn't shutting up either, going on about how emails get lost.

"Why don't you write down the one you have, and we'll see what that mix-up can be?" The judge smiled when Devon said he didn't have it on him right now. "Of course you don't."

"Your honor, I just want what I have coming to me as the son of Jacob Winslow. He's my father, and there should be something that you can do so that I get my fair share of his estate." The judge asked him if he wanted to go that route. "You mean, get it from my father's estate? Then yes, that's what I want to do."

After a small conference between Jake's attorney and Devon's, they sat back down. The attorney for Devon looked upset, but when he started putting his things in his briefcase, Devon took exception to that.

"What are you doing? You said that if I did this right, then they'd have to do what I want." The attorney whispered something to him. "No. I will not. You either help me or get out."

"Fine. Your honor, I've been dismissed from Mr. Winslow's service. If you wouldn't mind, I'd be happy not to go down with a sinking ship." The judge asked Devon if he wanted that. When Devon shooed him away, the younger man stood up. "If you wouldn't mind, your honor, I'd like to stick around and see how this ends. It might be the best case I've ever witnessed."

"Now, you want a part of the estate of Jacob Winslow, who is alive and kicking, because you think that his mother was on an allowance and she'd not have any to get. That's about right?" Devon said it was. "And you have a letter, signed and dated, from Jacob Winslow, that states that you're not only his son, but that he should have claimed you years ago. Also correct?"

"Yes. He's a good man who didn't deserve to have a son like Jake." The judge asked him what that meant. "Well, I'm not sure how you feel about it, but it truly disgusts myself and our father that Jake is a homosexual. And that man sitting next to him is also gay. I swear, if his mother knew, or his grandma, she'd be rolling over in her grave. It's not the right way things are to go."

"You the ruler of such things, are you?" Devon didn't look like he understood the question. "Never mind. But I will say

150

that this hearing has nothing to do with the sexual preference of Jake Winslow, but your claim on Jacob Winslow's estate."

"All right. But you have to admit, it's the grossest thing you've ever heard of." Devon looked at them and then back at the judge. "I think that people like them should be banned from inheriting anything."

"Be that as it may, we're here for something else." He picked up the yellow copy of the transcript. "Mr. Winslow, is it true that you visited Jacob yesterday at the prison? And that the two of you had a twenty-three-minute conversation about how you wanted him to sign off on the fact that he was your father, when you knew for certain that he wasn't?"

"No, I have the blood tests that will prove otherwise. How did you know that?" The judge told him how things were recorded. "You can't use that against me. That was a private conversation. That's not legal."

"It is. You were warned several times over the course of your visit that you'd be recorded. Also, Mr. Winslow sent the attorney that is here with Jake to his physician. Did you know what he had to say? That Jacob had a vasectomy. About a year and a half before you were born. And just the week before you would have been conceived, they're estimating, he was tested, and it was a good cut." He asked about the little girl. "Well, it's funny you should ask that. Just yesterday, it seems that Mr. Winslow, saying that he had nothing to lose, had a test done, and he is as fertile as a man half his age."

"This can't be happening to me." The judge asked him why not. "Because he slept with my mom all the time. He would knock her around, me too sometimes, but he never paid for it like the others did."

"Your mom was living in the home that Jacob provided

for her." Mr. Crenshaw approached the judge. "The rent was paid, as were the utilities. A phone was provided for her, insurance for her and Devon. She had an account at the local grocery store that she would charge all their food to, and he paid it as well. There are other charges as well that were made by Miss Rebecca Shiner, mother to Devon Shiner."

"The name isn't Jacob Winslow on the birth certificate as you told Jacob it was. Are you sure you don't want to call it a day, young man, and go home? It would more than likely cause you less grief if you did." Devon said that he wanted his father's estate. "Son, we've all but stuck you right here to see if you really are his son. It's just now working."

Mr. Crenshaw handed over another sheet of paper. Henry knew what this was. It was the DNA report from the restaurant. Even Devon was given a copy of it. It said with one hundred percent certainty that Jacob Winslow was not the father of Devon Shiner Winslow.

"How did you get that?" When he started to explain how it was taken, Devon had a fit. "No. You can't just take something that is mine and use it against me. That is not legal. I've seen something like that before."

"When Mr. Winslow here left the restaurant, he no longer was the owner of anything that he left behind. The chewing gum as well as the half-eaten pie was left there as property of the restaurant." The judge asked about the chain of command. "We had an FBI agent there, as well as two local police officers that served as witnesses. They signed the test bag as well as the paperwork that was sent in with it. As you can see, he isn't the son of anyone related to a Winslow."

Devon started screaming about illegally taking his samples. It was funny to Henry that the man just didn't know when to quit. He was still trying to get into Jacob's estate when Jake stood up and cleared his throat.

"Homo, just sit down." No one in the room moved; Henry was sure that you could hear a pin drop too. Devon looked around the room and sneered at them all. "He's taking it up the ass. You cannot really expect him to be around decent people. For Christ's sake, even his mom killed herself rather than be around him."

"I've had enough." The judge pounded on the desk when the room erupted in outrage. Not at Jake, as Devon had expected, but at him. "Take him to jail. I will not hear another word from him."

"Your honor, if you'd just give me one moment, I think I can help." The room once again was quiet. Devon asked what Jake thought he could do. "I'll give you all of my father's estate that belongs to him and my mother. Every bit of it."

"You'd do that?" Jake nodded. "Well all right, then. I guess being a gay hasn't affected your brain all that much yet, has it? How much is it? And when can I get it?"

~~~

Jake handed the paperwork to the judge. He had figured on doing this since late last week, when he'd heard that Devon only wanted his father's things. He'd outlined everything that his father owed and everything that his grandmother had given him over the years. The total amount had surprised him. Even the cost of Mom's funeral had been put on there as well. It amounted to well over a billion dollars that Jacob owed, since Jake's grandmother had been taking care of his parents.

"My father was a wealthy man. But only to those around him. Every cent he had, including the house and cars that he used, were only because my grandmother deemed him to have them." Devon said that wasn't right. "It is right. I have a list of everything she gave him, every receipt, as well as cash loans that Grandma meticulously wrote down. So please, let me finish. My father had nothing. Less than nothing. Grandma made the payments on his utilities, their trips, and even the plane that I now use. She had the money, not him. Grandma was a smart business woman, who taught me the meaning of saving money for a rainy day."

"So? What does this mean to me? You said you were going to give me the money from the estate." Jake reminded him that he could have whatever belonged to his father and mother. "And? How much is that?"

"Nothing. That's what I'm trying to tell you. There is no estate. There never was after my brother, Benny, was killed. Dad went on a gambling spree with Mom, and they lost it all. Every penny that they had, including the house that belonged to Grandma. Dad was a kept man. The estate that you want? It's now nothing but bills that need to be paid. My mom's funeral, even though it was private, cost more than your suit. There are no cars that he owns, no houses in other countries. Nothing at all that belonged to either of them."

"You lie." Jake said nothing. "There is no way that old broad would have been able to keep the money. There had to be more than whatever money she had. Right? What is it she left behind? I'm sure that it's not much."

"You want me to tell you what my Grandma's estate was? I can do that. But you're never going to get a dime of it. I won't pay for you to blackmail me." He asked him why not. "Because, and this is something that you should have understood by now—everyone here does—you're not a

154

Winslow. You never were, you never will be, and that's the end of it. And you're not going to inherit nor get anything from me or my family."

"You're not being fair. You have a lot of money, and you're gay." Jake asked him what that had to do with anything. "No one would leave you money if they knew what you were. Your grandma would have left it to a charity rather than have someone like you having it."

"She knew what I was long before my father murdered her. She also knew that my lover, who she's known for a long time since he was her attorney, was gay as well. And she loved me despite it." Jake laughed. "She thought it was a hoot that after being married to Carol, I'd found happiness with a friend of hers."

Devon lunged at him, but Jake only had to sidestep to get out of his way. Almost as soon as he hit the floor, the police and guards were on top of him. Watching them holding him down while he spewed obscenities was heart breaking for him. Jake didn't know why, but he did feel sorry for Devon. Just as he was ready to tell him he'd help, Forrest pulled him back.

"You do, and you'll never hear the end of him. Never. He'll be right there every day with his hand out, expecting you to not just fill it, but to carry him around on your back as well. Devon might not be related to your father, Jake, but he'll drain you like your father did his mom."

Jake nodded and stepped back. The people around them were getting an eye full today, he thought.

Devon was taken away. There would be charges pressed against him, enough that he'd be in jail for a long time, mostly for falsifying court documents. And knowingly lying to a judge. But Jake couldn't shake the feeling that he'd been just as much a victim as he'd been in this. He needed to do something. But what could he do that wouldn't have him doing just what Forrest had predicted? He'd have to give it some thought.

"Well, I don't know about you guys, but I'm all for a light dinner then home to bed. After I wash off the stink of today. That was.... Well, that's what it was, I guess. Insanely troubling, as well as enlightening about a lot of things." Henry laughed as he continued. "Some people are just thick headed, but he really was a solid ball there. I've never heard of anyone being more contrary than Devon was."

"Yes, I have to agree with you on that. And the fact that he just didn't want to believe anything but that he was my father's son is a little scary. I mean, seriously, why would you want to be?" Jake sat in the booth with the rest of them when they got to the pizza place. "I heard from Mary. She said that Jenna has been the best little girl today, but she thinks she misses us. I miss her too."

"She is a cutie. When she gets a little older, you're going to need to hire yourself a team to keep an eye on her and boys. Jenna is going to be a heartbreaker, I think."

Jake thought about what Paddy had said as they ordered. "Yes, well, having a tiger and a wolf around her all the time, it might make people think twice about trying to hurt her. She's going to be well protected, I think." Paddy told him not to forget about the pack. "Oh, I forgot to ask you about the job. Are you going to be the enforcer for Denny? I think it would be perfect for you."

"Yeah, we talked it over and I'm going to take it. And Henry is going to become a teacher for the pack as well.

He's going to work on helping the pack learn how to defend themselves when they're in the human world. Rather than shifting, he's going to help them fight to defend." Jake thought that was a wonderful idea. "Denny was all for it. And believe it or not, your streak leader would like for him to do the same. I understand that you two have become the attorneys for both of them as well."

"Yes, we're keeping it all in the family, apparently." Forrest held his hand under the table, and it felt good. Comfort wasn't something he was used to receiving, and he needed it today especially.

Jake and Forrest walked home after dinner. They were both exhausted, but being out and around their little town felt refreshing. They saw a lot of people that congratulated them on their win today, and a good many more that just wanted to thank them for being a part of the town. Jake wondered about that until Forrest explained.

"I hope you don't mind, but I volunteered us to hang out at the local food pantry. There are people there that could use some help with some small legal stuff, and William, the man who runs the place, said that the clients would be more apt to come to us in that sort of setting rather than at our office. Plus, it gets us out of the house." Jake said he thought it was a good idea. "I thought you'd say that. I have a buddy that I've called too. He's a retired doctor. Not down on his luck or anything, but just a lonely man. He retired about a year ago when his partner died in a horrific car accident. He is coming to help out with us, to see about medical help for some of the people there."

"Does he have a mate?" Forrest laughed and said he didn't. But he was a nice man. "The reason I ask is, we've got a good thing going here, what with calling in help and finding a mate. Not that it matters, but is he by chance gay as well?"

"He is. Like you, he's only just figured it out. But he's very reserved about his homosexuality. Not really comfortable with it. But he'll come around. Especially hanging out with the four of us." Jake nodded and said he hoped so. "When Jenna is a little older, I thought that we'd take a trip abroad. I've not been anywhere all that special in a long time. I was thinking we could go to New York, see a play or two, and do some shopping. Christmas is in a few months, and it might be a good time for us to see about finding some furniture for the other rooms we emptied out. What do you think?"

"Splendid. I think Grandma left us a nice place downtown. It's a big five-bedroom place. We should see if Mary wants to hang out with us, as well as Henry and Paddy. And Christy would love it as well. We could have fun with her, taking her to plays and galleries. Everyone could probably use a break." Forrest said that would be wonderful. "All right. I'll see about getting the place aired out and get some food put in. I've never been there, but I bet it's nice. Grandma had excellent taste."

"She did. Just look at how she liked both of us." They were laughing when they entered their home. Jake was so happy that they'd moved here, leaving the other house to someone that could brighten it up. After the deaths that had occurred there, he knew it needed happiness. And Paddy and Henry were perfect for the job.

Mary said that he had a phone message, and he didn't want to bother with it now. But she told him it was the prison, and they'd said that it was important that he call them. Nodding, he wondered if his father had died or something, and went to make the call in his office. Putting the call through, all he could think about was that his father was ruining his day yet again.

Chapter 11

Paddy moaned when warm hands spread over his back. He'd tried his best to be quiet when he woke up, letting Henry sleep as late as he wanted. He'd not been sleeping well, and no matter how much he tried to talk to him about it, Henry wouldn't tell him what was going on.

"You have the nicest back. I'm assuming that when you shift, there are no scars either." He told him he healed quickly, and the only scars he had were small ones made by another wolf. "I love touching you. Let me wash your back, but don't turn around. I need to talk to you."

"All right. But I want you to know that whatever it is, or you think it is, I either won't care or we can fix it." Henry kissed him on the shoulder as the warm brush touched his back. "Tell me, Henry. I'm really worried about you."

"Okay. I have a part." He started to turn but Henry held him to the wall. "Just let me tell you about it before you talk. I have a part, a big part in an upcoming movie. It's worldwide, this movie will be, and I'd have to go out to Hollywood for a

161

few months. I know that we've both just started our new jobs, but I would like to talk to you about taking it."

"You should." Henry said he wasn't finished. "All right. But I know that you loved acting, and I'd love to go to Hollywood with you. I've never been anywhere but around Ohio. Not that it's not a great state, but I just never was able to afford to do much."

"You'd just drop everything and go with me?" He turned then. The shocked look on Henry's face gave him an idea what had been keeping him up at nights. Paddy nodded. "I thought you'd tell me to have a good time, or worse, to not go or lose you."

"You have a lot to learn about mates, and me apparently." Henry shook his head, his emotions right there on his face. "You shouldn't have let this bother you. Come and talk to me and we can work things out. Wherever you go, I will be there with you. And even if you don't want me to be, I'll snuggle up with you in the middle of the night when you've had such a bad day that all you want to do is cry. Just like you did for me."

"Wally said that you needed me, and I went. He got me into your hotel room too. He's very resourceful." Paddy would have to thank the old man. "You and I, we're okay then? I mean, this part, it could be big or nothing at all."

"It'll be huge, and you know it." He told him who the director was. "Wow, that is going to be huge. I may not know anything about acting, but even I recognize his name. This is fantastic. When do you have to leave?"

"After the next couple of months. Maybe sooner if they can get all the actors together at once. I was told it would probably be right after the new year. I guess he's anticipating no one wanting to leave their homes around the holidays. I'm so glad you're going with me. I don't know if I could have stayed focused without you being there." Paddy hugged him, and then kissed the only man that he'd ever love. "And this will help me relax as well. I've been so nervous."

"Don't do that again." Paddy dropped to his knees and kissed the tip of his cock. "Promise me, from now on you talk to me about this kind of thing. I don't like you being tense."

"I promise. Holy fuck, yes." Paddy wrapped his mouth around him and held his warm skin. He loved this guy, and wanted to show him how much in every way possible.

Touching him everywhere he could reach, tasting him while he fucked his mouth slowly, Henry made him feel like a man on top of the world. He loved the way that he responded to him. The sounds that he made when he was close. Even the hitch in his breath when he was moaning made Paddy want more.

Taking his heavy sacs in his hands, he gave them a slight squeeze. It was all it took for him to come, and come hard. When he was ready to stand, Henry jerked him up from the floor and pressed him against the tile. Paddy felt his cock twist painfully in a good way as soon as he took him.

The coupling was quick but so satisfying. Each time they made love, every time they touched, it was like being renewed. Paddy had had a few lovers in his lifetime, but none of them had ever made him feel like Henry did. Not just loved, though that was there in abundance, but appreciated and respected as well.

They showered then, washing each other, touching as well. Wolves were a cuddle group. They liked to be touched and to touch. Henry had gotten used to that quickly, and he was enjoying it as much as Paddy did now.

Getting dressed and making plans, he told him about the luggage that he'd found in the attic. Henry wondered if Jake had any idea that there were things up there, and they decided to have a look. It was well after time for breakfast, and they decided to have an early lunch instead. The attic held a lot of excitement for them both.

As soon as they entered, he knew that Jake hadn't ever been up there. The things that were around were dusty, and cobwebs were on everything. He looked at the trunks that were as old as he'd ever seen, and went for those. Henry was looking at the box of old albums.

"Look, there's a record player too. We need to take this downstairs and use it. I love the scratchy sound of albums." Paddy told him that he had a large cd selection at his apartment. "Oh, that's being packed up. Your landlord is letting the men come in and pack it up this weekend. I forgot to tell you. I figured you and I could go through it as you wanted. There's plenty of room in the garage to store it."

"Thanks." He unlocked the first trunk with the key that hung on a lovely chain that was wrapped around it. "I don't have any idea, but having the thing locked with the key right here makes me slightly nervous. Like that old movie where they locked the monster in the trunk and then buried it? That's an old movie."

"I think I might have seen it." They were both laughing when he opened the trunk up. Paddy could only stare at the contents, and wondered why it had never been found before. Then just as he was going to touch the old uniform, Henry said his name quietly. "He's here. The man I think that it belongs to."

Paddy looked at him as he stood over the trunk. He couldn't have been any more than eighteen or nineteen years old. He'd been shot, he could see, and it had hit him on his forehead and came out the back. Paddy asked him if it was his.

"My brother's. He was never found." Paddy told him how sorry he was. "I visit him daily, but he wants to come home. On the backside of this property, there is an overgrown cemetery. I'm there, but not Howie. I don't much know how that's gonna work, with it being so long now."

"We can help you with that, if you want." He nodded. "I don't understand how this came to be in this house. The house isn't nearly old enough for you to have lived here. If I know my uniforms well enough, I think you might be from World War I, correct?"

"Yes. My brother and I, we went away at the same time. He was all hyped up to join and see the world, and I went along to be with him. My name is Grant. Grant Sheppard. Howie, he's been waiting for a very long time. He was killed in nineteen fifteen. My death was a few days after I landed off the boat, in nineteen fourteen." Paddy told him he was sorry. "Can you really help him? Howie knows that everyone is dead now, I think."

"Where is he? I mean, is he buried someplace or just there?" Paddy had a feeling that he wasn't buried at all. That would be why he'd not been sent home. It must have cost the family to have one son sent home back then. "This house belonged to someone in your family, Grant?"

"My cousin, I think he was. He.... I don't know him at all. He lived here for a very short time after my trunk was given to him. I tried very hard to get him to get Howie, but I think

I might have been too much. He left here in the middle of the night, leaving everything behind." Grant grinned. "He wasn't a nice person. Nor was the woman that lived here before you. She was a terrible individual, I'm sorry to say, and I stayed away from her."

"I never met her, but I heard some stories about her that would curl your toes." Grant laughed with him. "She's passed on now. I've not seen her lurking around, but if you do, let us know so we can hide too."

"Grant, I can call him here if he doesn't have a marker. Does he have one?" Howie said that he was left where he died, in the middle of a battlefield. "I can summon him here. I can't have him buried, but the two of you could stay here in our home should you want. We don't mind at all."

"No, it would be wonderful to talk to you about your life." Paddy had a sudden idea that he wanted to write about the two men. "We'll have Howie come here, and you two can visit us as much as you'd like. There is a young woman, she lives here too. She's my sister."

"Christy. I have met her. She is a delight. And so honest in her talking to me. I have told others about her and what she can do to help. Some of us older ones, we don't need to leave, but it's nice having someone to talk to. She has such a beautiful smile." Paddy thanked him. "If you could summon my Howie, that would be wonderful, sir."

Paddy looked at Henry. He'd have better luck at this than he would. While he thought of the way he'd been told by Wally that it had to be done, he knew that there was a step or two that he'd not been told about. Paddy wondered if it would bring some kind of demon to them if he had done it his way.

166

It took a little longer than he thought it would. But while they sorted through the other trunk with pictures and other small items in it, he watched Grant. The deeper he dug into the parts of their lives in the boxes inside the trunk, the more he wanted to write this book. And when Howie appeared in the room with them, Paddy realized why he couldn't leave his brother. They were identical twins.

"Thank you so much." The two of them got as close as they could without touching. He knew that the dead couldn't interact with the living, but he'd not realized the same rules applied with the dead. Grant looked at him and told him thanks again for opening the trunk. "You've brought us together again. I would do anything for you."

"I want to write a book." He glanced at Henry, and when he nodded at him, he felt encouraged. "I'd like to write a book about the two of you. Your war stories, as well as your family life. I think it would be a good thing, since the two of you gave your lives for our country. And I'd like to use these pictures if I may. We brought you together because it was the right thing to do. But if you'd rather I didn't, then I can understand that as well."

"We're not nobody important, you know." Paddy told Howie that they were to them. "I don't mind none if Grant don't." When the other man shook his head, Paddy was excited to get started. "You go on and think up what you wanna ask us, young man, and we'll be there for you. But if you don't mind, we'd like to just talk for a bit. When I'd go to visit him, there wasn't any way for us to do much more than stare at each other and be lonely."

"Of course. I'm betting you have a lot to catch up on. Grant, is your family buried here as well? I mean, parents and other brothers or sisters?" He said that they were all here, but he'd not seen them. "Okay. We'll take a walk back there soon. Maybe my sister would like to join us, so she can meet Howie."

"I'd surely like that." They faded out, just like they did in the movies, and were gone. Paddy sat there for several minutes just thinking about the book he was going to try and do. Turning to Henry, he asked him how to begin.

"I'd say when they moved to this area. Or their parents did." Paddy said that wasn't what he meant. "I know that, but you can do this. And you'll do a great job of it. It'll be so true to life that everyone will want you to write their stories too. There are some pretty messed up things in the world of the deceased."

Digging deeper into the first trunk, he found some items that he was sure didn't belong to either man. It was a small tea set that looked brand new, as well as some other things that were very little girlish. Paddy wondered aloud if they'd had a little sister. These were things that he was going to make it a point to ask them about. Trying to keep them all straight was making him nuts until Henry handed him an old notebook and a pen. He started writing things down immediately.

"You know, even if it doesn't sell a single copy, I'm very happy to be doing this. It's like I'm going to be a voice for the dead." Paddy laughed when Henry did. "Too sappy, but I am excited to begin this. It'll keep me out of trouble, I think."

"More than likely not."

He was still writing things down when they were in the kitchen an hour later. Paddy was thinking about the things that he'd need to make this work; the first thing would be a computer.

~~~

Quincey was waiting for them on the porch when they returned from their walk. Even the baby had gone along, and he was excited to finally meet her. He was also going to talk to Jake and tell him what he should have told his grandma long ago.

"Hello. I'm so happy to see you today. We have such news." Jake hugged him. It was the first time in longer than Quincey could remember that someone had hugged him without asking first. "There's a cemetery at the back of the property we sold Paddy and Henry, did you know that?"

"I did. I knew the family too when they were alive. I think they're all gone now." Paddy mentioned the cousin or something that had lived in Jake's house. "Oh, yes. I think he's gone as well now. He didn't take good care of himself."

Paddy told him that he was going to write a book on the family. Also, about the trunks he'd found, and how Henry had summoned one of the brothers home. He was so excited that Quincey was happy for him.

"The Sheppards might have been the first family in the area. I'm not sure. But there were a lot of them. The mother had several sisters, and all of them married local men here. The two boys that you're talking about, I remember them as well. Nice kids. Too bad that they died so young." Paddy said he was going to use the pictures that were with the uniform as well. "It'll be a best seller. I think there might be a scandal or two that I can tell you. Also, a love affair. Not with me, but with the local mayor at the time."

Henry and Paddy went to their home a little while later, saying that they had some shopping to do for a computer and such. Quincey thought that Paddy would do a very good job with the story, and was happy that someone that he knew was going to be putting it to paper.

"Okay, all the niceties are out of the way. What's going on?" Quincey laughed at Jake, so much like his grandmother that he missed her just a little less when around him. "Have you something you need for us to do? You've only to ask and I'll take care of it."

"I heard that you're to visit your father." He nodded, looking sad for a moment. "You don't have to go, Jake. There is more than likely nothing he could say that would make you change your mind about him."

"No, nothing will. But he asked to see me, politely I might add, and I'm going to do it. I've already told the man who called that I wasn't taking his shit, nor was I paying for him an attorney. He can, and more than likely will, rot in hell for all I care." Quincey only nodded. The boy had no idea of the extent of his father's crimes. "All right. Spill it."

"I'm your great grandfather." He let that sink in, and when Jake didn't ask questions, Quincey asked if he'd heard him. "I'm your grandfather, did you hear me?"

"I knew that. You are my grandma's father." He nodded. "Grandma knew, and told me about it. She wasn't sure why you never told her, but she knew it, I think."

"You're part vampire?" Jake nodded at Forrest when he asked. "That'll change a few things then. I had no idea when we were talking about you being changed into a tiger."

"You can do it. You should do it. But why I'm here telling you this today is, I've decided that I don't want things to go unsaid between us." Forrest picked up little Jenna and Quincey asked to hold her. "She only has a small part of me inside of her, just enough to make her healthy and heal quickly. But you, Jake, you are nearly just like me."

Jake shook his head even as Quincey nodded. Quincey didn't want to frighten either of them, but he could see that they needed a bit more convincing before he took away his protection. Quincey asked for them both to have a seat.

"I've been protecting you since the day you were born. I've not always stepped in when you needed me to. I thought that to over protect you would mean that you'd fail. Or worse yet, become like your father was." Jake thanked him for that. "So, since you were born, you've had protective magic surrounding you. It was to keep you from needing as much as I did until you were at a point where you could handle it."

"You mean that I'm a vampire." It wasn't a question for him to answer, but he told him that he was. Or nearly so. "How much is nearly so? I mean, when this magic is gone— I'm assuming that you can do that—but when it's gone, will I become someone that drinks blood and feeds off humans?"

"You'd normally be able to feed from humans. But not now that you have a mate. You can only feed from him." Jake was taking this well, and so was Forrest. But he might just be in shock. "You have what I have. Magic, as well as long life. And when you took a mate, Forrest, you gave the same gift to him."

"Did my grandma have it, this magic?" Quincey said that for decades he'd tried to get her to let him change her, but she said that when her time came, she wanted it to come so she could go to her husband. "That sounds like her."

"What your father did to her, shooting her like he did, she would not have survived it anyway, I'm sorry to say. And not because she was shot, but because she only got a small part of me when she was conceived. Very small." He looked down at his granddaughter. "Jenna has more, but not much. She will have a very long life too. And when she meets her mate, she'll pass it to him."

"You say long life. But I have a feeling that it's more than just a few decades longer than normal, isn't it?" Quincey nodded. "How much longer?"

"You're an immortal. The same as I am. And so is Forrest." Jake nodded again, then took Forrest's hand in his when he reached for him. "Do you need me to answer any questions? Or do you want me to slow down?"

"I'm not sure. Just give me a minute." Quincey told him to take as much time as he needed. "My grandma was your daughter. Where is her mother? I'm assuming that she wasn't a vampire."

"No." Quincey laughed. "She was a tiger. Pure blood, same as Forrest is. That's what your sister is as well. Mostly tiger."

"Christ, this is like a circle of news, isn't it?" They all laughed with Forrest. "Okay, so Mom is a tiger, Dad a vampire. Why didn't Grandma have any of these traits? Or for that matter, Jacob. Why was he just plain old Jacob and nothing more? Or was he?"

"He was nothing more than the asshole man that he is now." Jake said thank goodness. "Yes, I agree with you there. Your grandma, as I said, had more of the tiger in her, as well as my traits. She was healthy, as you can attest to. Strong minded, which is scary true, but her DNA wasn't nearly as receptive of the magic that we both held. It was there, but dormant."

"I had a brother. Benny. What was he? And why do I have a feeling that his accident was more than that?" Quincey had

172

hoped that this wouldn't be brought up now, but there was no hope for it. "You know something about his death."

"I do. He was more tiger. And on the day that he died, it wasn't as your parents had been told. He wasn't on a bike, but in a wooded area when he shifted for the first time. It terrified him, as you can well imagine, but before I could go to him, to help him with this change, he killed himself. Hung himself because he didn't want to be imperfect. He knew that his father and mother would never approve." Jake asked if they had known about any of it. "I don't know, to be honest. I hadn't been aware that Benny could shift either. His tiger DNA was very small. Less than one percent of his makeup, but he was a troubled young man. Even before that."

"He was into drugs." Quincey nodded at Jake. "I had no idea either, not until we were going through some of Grandma's things. There is a report from a doctor in a clinic outside the state that Benny had been to for drugs. Then another place for alcohol addiction. There is also a copy of his death certificate with her things. They found a lot of drugs in his system, as well as other things."

"I had no idea that your grandmother knew that."

Jake nodded and got up to pace. Quincey watched Jake. He knew this was a lot to throw at him right now, but he wanted him to be prepared for his visit with his father. He was going to say hurtful things to him, and Quincey would rather he heard it from him than the man who had killed his only child.

"My father and mother always threw it in my face how I was the imperfect child for them. That they wished it had been me that was killed that day, and not their precious Benny. And all this time, he was as messed up as I was." Jake stopped and looked at him. "My father. This is why he wants to see me tomorrow."

"I don't know what he knows, to be honest. I have an idea that he's done some investigating into the death of Benny. I cannot read his mind, I never could. But I have found out recently that he'd made some inquiries about things that are associated with his death, and that could be what he is going to tell you about. Not about Benny being a drug addict, but about other things, things that he'll hope to hurt you with."

Jake paced again, talking to himself. Quincey looked at Forrest and asked him if he was all right.

"I am. I've been dealing with shifters all my life. And even though he knows some, he doesn't know a great deal about our kind. Neither does Henry, but they're learning." Quincey said that he could send someone to help them both. "I might take you up on that. I have a lot to learn myself, I think. Paddy is a wolf. I know nothing at all about them."

When Jake sat down, he looked determined. Like he knew that whatever he said next was going to be well thought out and clear. Just like his grandmother, Quincey thought. She never uttered a word without a great deal of thought about it.

Chapter 12

Jacob waited for his son to show up. He had a list of things he was going to inform him of, starting with how his own sainted grandmother wasn't as nice nor as pure as she'd let them all think she was. Looking down at the paper, he was almost giddy to think that he'd been holding this for so long, and now, after the old cunt was gone, he was no longer being held to an unbreakable rule. You tell him, you will die a starving, broken man.

His own mother had actually said that to them. Telling them that Jake was the only one that understood her and needed her, especially as cold hearted and cruel as his own parents, her son even, was to him all the time. She even told them all about Benny and how he'd actually died. There was no way that his son was anything like one of those things. He was a good boy who Jake had never taken care of.

Jacob was told he had a visitor and he stood up, ready to get this done. His trial was in a few days, Monday as a matter of fact, and he knew there wasn't going to be any help from his friends. Once they'd discovered what he'd done, they had shunned him as harshly as any Quaker would their own.

Jake was waiting for him when he was seated. Jacob hated that he got to see him chained to the floor and the table. Usually, with his attorney, he was seated and locked in before he came to him. This was unexpected, and it pissed him off even more than he already was.

Jake picked up the phone when he did. So, it was going to be like this, was it? He wasn't going to be any more cooperative now than he had been when he was younger. Jacob didn't like Jake. He'd always been a great disappointment to him and his wife.

"What did you want?" Jacob didn't like the way he spoke to him and said as much. "Like I care what you like. What do you want, Father? I've come here, and whatever it is, tell me so I can go on with my life."

"You're an ungrateful cur, did you know that?" He started to hang up and Jacob stood up as far as he could, telling him to sit down. He did, but even through the glass, he could feel his anger. "You will sit there and listen to me until I'm finished. Then you can go on with your life, whatever that might be."

"I have your daughter. Jenna is a beautiful little girl, despite being related to you." He said she wasn't his. "As sorry as I am to tell you this, she is. I've read up on vasectomies, and they don't last forever on some men. Especially as long ago as you had yours. Right after I was born, I guess."

"Who told you that?" Jake only smiled at him. "Well, I'd like proof before I acknowledge her. You see that I get it."

"I have, and your acknowledging her matters shit to anyone. She might even decide that she doesn't want to be related to you after she reads about you later in life." His hatred for his son doubled in that moment. "By the way, I've also been informed about Benny. He wasn't as perfect as you always made me think he was. A drug addict. Drunk all the time. What made you think — ?"

"You will not spew those lies to me. Do you hear me? He was a saint compared to you." Jacob was told to calm down or he was going back to his cell. The guard with him even put his hand on his Taser to make sure he understood he was serious. Taking a few calming breaths, he looked at Jake again. "You will never speak of that to anyone. It's all lies."

The bills from the clinic were pressed against the glass. The doctor's report was there as well. He didn't have to read it to know what it said. He had it memorized. The doctors said that Benny had left without permission. His treatments were far from over. It also said that if he didn't get treatment soon, and didn't stay away from all the things he'd been taking and doing, drugs and alcohol, he was going to die.

"And what does this prove to me? That you know how to snoop around in things that don't concern you? You're no better than your grandmother." Jake thanked him. "It wasn't meant to be a compliment, you moron. I didn't like her any more than I do you."

"You mean because she was a product of a vampire and a tiger? Or was there something else that you hated? Was it because she wouldn't just die and leave the money to you? I think that is what you hated most. That she was better at managing.... Well, she was better at managing anything than you were." Jacob looked down at his notes. Nothing was going well. Every point that he had decided to inform his son about, he was throwing it in his face. "You see, I've been doing some checking, or snooping as you call it, myself. I know a great deal about you and what you were."

"And what was I other than a damned good father to you?" Jake laughed. "You're not still pissed off about Carol, are you? You got that taken care of, didn't you? Or she did it for you. Hung herself instead of staying married to you. And now look at you. A faggot. A freak of nature that has no more right to be breathing than any of the other monsters you hang around with. Yes, I remember what he is. He nearly took my throat out."

"I wish he had." Jake stood up and put the phone in the cradle. When Jacob tried to as well to tell him he wasn't finished yet, he had to stoop over again, the chains on his wrists and ankles making it impossible for him to stand up to his son. Picking up the phone again when Jake did, he started to tell him to sit when he spoke first. "Chained like a monster is just what you deserve."

Then he was gone. Hung up the phone with a gentle hand and turned and walked away. Jacob was told to sit down again, his body straining hard against the chains to go after Jake and show him just what a monster he was.

"Jacob, if you don't sit down right now, I'm going to hurt you." He sat down, but in that moment, he did hurt. And it was his heart. His son had.... Jacob looked at the guard who he didn't know, and felt tears falling down his face. "Jacob?"

"What have I done? Who have I become?" Without a word, he was unchained and taken back to his cell. Jacob was handed his note, the one that he'd been so proud of only an hour ago. Looking at it now, he realized that he was just what he'd called his son. A monster.

Jacob realized then that he was alone. Not only in his cell, but in life. There would be no one to sit in the courtroom hoping for his release. When he died, there would be no grievers, no one to sit in a funeral room and bemoan his passing. He doubted too that he'd have a single flower, or a card of condolence. There would be no one to receive them if he did.

It was too late for him. And he knew that he had caused it all, that he'd pushed and pushed until there was no one left. Jacob got up from the bed, his only bed for a very long time, and walked around his little cell.

He realized also that this was just like his home. Cold, and nothing here was his. Not anything that he picked out or even cared about. Jacob sat down on the floor of the cell and backed himself into the corner.

Here he sat, fifty-seven years old. He'd had money at one time, his own. He'd owned homes all over the world. Money to spend when he wanted something. And a beautiful wife and two sons. Boys that, while not what he would have picked out for himself, were his. His addition to the world as a whole.

At one time he had thought of grandchildren. A child that would come to him and hug him. This was before the boys were born, and his wife was carrying their first child. Dreams of a swing set in the back yard. Trips with them to faraway places, even if it was only in the back yard. Those thoughts and dreams soon faded to the background. He'd seen what children did to people, his own doing the same to him.

Now, in a moment of desperation, he had lost it all. But if he really thought about it — and since he had nothing else to do, he did — Jacob had been losing it all for a long time. Life had chipped away his lifestyle. Whittled away his money and his happiness. And he was the only person he could blame for that. He'd fucked up, royally, and even though he'd been a mean bastard to her, his mom had always been there for him.

Jacob had hated the way she'd lorded things over him. But she hadn't. There were rules and he had to follow them. He thought now that he hated the way she'd treated him as a child. He had been one. Having temper tantrums every time things didn't go his way. Now she was gone, by his hand, and he'd never be able to tell her how very sorry he was.

Jake had been right about a lot of things about him. Over the years his son had tried very hard to have him in his life. But after Benny died — after Benny had killed himself — he had lost interest in even the smallest of things. He and Trina had drifted apart and gone their separate ways in a lot of things. And he knew that she'd been suffering, her depression getting the better of her more and more of late. Twice in the last year before she killed herself, she had tried to end her life; once taking a drug overdose, the second time slicing her wrists. Jacob sobbed now for what he'd told her about that.

"You can't even kill yourself properly. You cut yourself the wrong way, Trina. How on earth you stayed alive for this long without me is beyond anything I've ever known." But she'd gotten it right the last time. Had walked away from him and into the bathroom and done it.

He should have asked for help. Should have gone to his mother and told her that Trina was ill, that he needed the money to have someone keep an eye on her. Perhaps give her something to help her cope with life. But he'd been pissed and ashamed that he would need to beg, even for her.

"I killed her. Just the same as if I had sliced her wrists on my own."

Leaning his head back against the cold concrete, he

thought about Jake and his growing up. He had been a model son. Following in his footsteps to become a lawyer. But the difference was, Jake had worked at his craft. He had become a good attorney, and knew what he was doing. Secretly Jacob had kept up with his career, hoping, he knew back then, to see somehow that he'd failed. But he hadn't, not once. There had been no scandal, except the one that his wife had caused.

That had been another mistake...selling his son to the Lanes. He had wanted the money to pay back his mother, to get on her better side, marry his son off and out of his life, but it never worked out that way. The money came in, like it was supposed to, but it never made it to the bank for bills. It went to things like shopping sprees. Lavish trips abroad. And for what? Nothing tangible to show for what he'd done.

An unhappy son. A bitch of a daughter-in-law that he hated more than he thought he had Jake, and no grandchildren. Jacob hadn't been aware that was what he wanted from them, a child, but he hadn't gotten any, and that saddened him now. There was no one.

"Mr. Winslow?" He looked up at the man. Not having any idea who he was, he just stared at him. "My name is Patrick Garrett. I'm a friend of your son's. Wally, another friend, sent me here. It should have been Henry, but he's away right now, getting the contracts signed on.... It doesn't matter. I was sent here by Wally."

"How did you get in here?" He said magic. "Of course. Magic. I guess there are more people out there with it than I thought."

"I suppose. You need me to help you, right?" He asked him for what. "To talk to your mother and son."

~~~

181

They were both there, Jenna and Benny. The younger man looked like his mother, and not so much like his dad. And Jake looked like neither of them. He was glad for that. The man on the floor looked hard and unapproachable.

"Wally is a ghost that helps us sometimes. He's been talking to your mom, and she has been here, I guess. She wants to tell you something." Jacob didn't look like he was going to go along with this. Paddy wasn't even sure he could do this alone. But Wally said that Jenna wanted to talk to her son, and he'd do anything for the woman that Jake had so much love for.

"You can see ghosts. And talk to them. Is this a joke? Has Jake sent you here to torment me?" He said that Jake hadn't any idea he was here. "He hates me."

"I'm not sure why you'd think he shouldn't. You're a bastard and a prick." Jacob nodded. "Do you want to talk to your mom or not? And Benny, he has something to say to you as well. You can't ask them to do anything for you, and they know the rules as well as I do about that. And if I mess up, Wally is here to help me."

"You know I don't believe you, don't you?" Paddy stood up. "No. Please, don't leave. I don't.... I've been sitting here feeling sorry for myself and realizing what a real bastard I've been. Please, help me."

"All right. First off, no one can see me. If someone comes in here and talks to you, you can't tell them I'm here. Nor the ghosts. I'm here because Quincey helped me. He doesn't like you either, so you know. In the event you don't know who he is, he's your grandfather." Jacob said that he knew who he was. "All right then. Jenna is here, but Benny is fading faster. His body has been cremated, and it's harder for him to hold his shape. So, he wants me to tell you what he has to say, all right?"

"Yes, all right. How does he look?" Paddy told him that he looked like he'd hung himself. "Yes, of course. He did, you know. When no one helped him. Not even me."

"Dad, shut up." Paddy laughed when he told Jacob what Benny said and his mouth snapped closed. "You're a bastard, even to me. And when you and Mom had that party when I was eight, you were the one that gave me my first drink, my introduction into drugs and the lifestyle that eventually got me killed. Yes, I did hang myself, but it wasn't because I shifted as people think. I killed myself because it was a joke. I was trying to impress a girl. The note that you got, it wasn't written by my hand, but hers. They didn't want you to know that I killed myself by accident."

Jacob cried then. Sobbed like a man who had lost something huge. Paddy asked Benny if there was anything else, and he nodded. When Jacob looked at him, he could see the pain of this etched on his face. Jacob looked like he had aged twenty years in the last few minutes.

"Tell him that I love and forgive him for what he did to me. But I can't for what he's done to Jake. Jake was a good kid, and a better adult than I ever would have been. He was there for me, even when you shoved him away or compared him to me. When in reality, you should have been saying those things to me about him. Jake was my hero." Benny started to fade away, but came back to say one more thing. "Tell him I forgive him."

Paddy felt drained. The words were truthful, yes, but cruel and hurtful. He wondered if given the chance he'd say the same to his own father. But his had only been absent, not a horrific person like this man was.

When Jenna stood next to him, she touched her fingers to his head. He could almost feel it, the warmth of her love, but he knew that couldn't be right...she didn't know him at all. Other than something she might have gotten when she'd contacted him before her death. Paddy looked at her and asked her if she was ready.

"I am. But I would like to say that I'm forever around. Watching and keeping an eye on my boys. That includes you and Henry now as well. You're a good man. And I'm so proud of you for what you're doing with Howie and Grant." He said that he was having fun talking to them, getting to know their life story. "You will do a good job for them, and many people will be happy to read it."

"Is that my mother?" He nodded at Jacob, seeing the man in a new light today. Not that he liked him any better, but he had come to some kind of understanding about things. "I'd like to talk to her. Please?"

"Tell him that when I'm ready. The little shit killed me. The least he can do is be nicer to me." Paddy told him what she'd said, and she laughed when Jacob nodded. "I don't think I've ever heard him say please quite like that before. As if he actually means it. And doing what I want? Well, I shall remember this day for a long while."

"I'm sorry, Mother." She looked at him and then at Jacob as he continued. "I don't know where I went wrong or how, but I was wrong. About a great many things about you, and how you were with Jake. He wouldn't have been half the man he is without you in his life."

Jacob never looked up. He stared at his lap the entire time he spoke to his mom. Jenna said very little too, just watching

184

Jacob as he cried again. When she moved toward Jacob now, Paddy said nothing. He wanted to wait and see what happened.

"Benny was so much like me. He was a bastard and a shit. Just like you told me he was. And even though I treated you like shit, you still went out of your way to make sure that he had a nice funeral, and you even went so far as to keep everything out of the paper about why he had ended his life." She told him that she'd not known it was a joke. "It wouldn't have mattered. Not to you. You would still have done what you did. Taken care of everything when we just couldn't. At the time, I felt as if you had taken even that away from me. But there wasn't any way that either of us, Trina or I, would have been able to plan and execute the funeral for him."

"It wasn't because of you, Jacob, but for Jake. He hurt so badly, and you just tossed him aside, like he was nothing more to you than an inconvenience that you'd just as soon get rid of as to love." He said that he knew that. "And then what did you do? You sold him off to that horrid woman, just because you thought that she'd kill him. I don't have it in my heart to forgive you, Jacob. Not because of what you did and said to me, but for what you did to that little boy. He'd just lost the only brother he had, and you didn't even let him hug you."

"I remember, just like it was yesterday, what I said to him that day. I blamed him for his brother's death. I even told him that I wished it was him instead of Benny. I was a monster." Jenna told him that he still was. "Yes, I am. I know that now. I'm all alone, Mother. I don't know how that happened."

"Yes you do. You took a good thing, which was life, and you threw it all away for the prestige of money. And what did that give you, Jacob? Did you have friends that you could count on? A son that you could just say, come and visit me, I've fucked up and I need for you to forgive me? He won't, in the event you haven't figured that out by now. Benny forgave you, but he didn't know you like we did. Hadn't seen you in action over the last ten years or so. We know you better. And I will not forgive you."

Paddy wanted her to do just that. To tell the man, her son, that she did forgive him. Even if they were words for him and not herself. But he also knew something that he'd never tell Jacob. It was hurting Jenna as much as it was Jacob to tell him the truth. Inside, Jenna was hurting as badly, if not worse than her son was.

Jacob laid on his cot and cried harder. Paddy wasn't sure what he was supposed to do now. Jenna was still there, but it looked to him like she'd said all she wanted to her son. But when Jacob asked him if she'd left, Jenna asked him what he wanted now.

"I know that you can't forgive me. But I'd like for you to do one thing for me. Please. I wish for you to watch over my children for me." She told him she was doing that anyway. "I guess I know that as well. But they'll need a good guiding hand in the future, and I would rest better knowing that you're watching them."

"What do you suppose he's planning on doing?" Paddy asked him the question. But instead of an answer, Jacob laid back down. He was no longer crying, and for some reason that scared him a little too. "If he kills himself, I'm going to be royally pissed off at him. Tell him that."

He did, and waited for some sort of reaction from Jacob. But all he did was lay there. Not moving other than his breaths in his chest. He continued to stare up at the ceiling as Jenna screamed at him to get up, he was not going to kill himself.

The anger took its toll on Jenna. When she could no longer hold onto her body, she left them there. Jacob didn't move when he told him she was gone, nor did he say anything when he asked if he could help him in anyway. Just as he was turning to leave, Jacob finally spoke.

"Don't tell Jake that you were here. Not that I think he'd care, but don't tell him. And if you see my mother again, tell her that I'm not going to kill myself. I've made my bed, and now I know that I must lie in it." Paddy said that he would. "Also, thank you, young man. I don't know why you came here to help me, when it's more than likely I would never have done a thing to help you. But I do thank you. From the bottom of my cold black heart."

Paddy called to Quincey. The man appeared in front of him in seconds. But instead of taking him home, where he desperately wanted to be, he hugged him, tightly, in his arms until it was almost painful. And before he could stop himself, Paddy started crying for the loss of love between these people. It was so profound that he was limp with it.

When he was released, he was back at his home. Quincey asked him if he was all right to leave alone now, and Paddy told him he wasn't sure. Quincey laughed and said he'd more than likely have the same answer.

"Your entire family is…well, for the most part, fucked up, wouldn't you say?" He laughed when Paddy did. "I mean, you have a grandson, some kind of great grandson, raising his sister as his own. You have another grandson in prison for killing off your daughter. You've lost your wife somewhere along the line, I'm assuming. And you have a bunch of

187

homosexual men using your magic to try and make everyone happy."

"Are you? Happy, I mean. Are you happy, Patrick?" He said that he was getting there. "You should be very happy. You have more than most being a homosexual man these days. A lover, friends. A successful career, as well as another one that you're pursuing. There are a great many people out there that wish they had half what you have."

"I'm sorry. You must think I'm a bastard." Quincy shook his head and said that he'd never think that of him. "Then what did you mean?"

"What do you think you can do to make others successful? I don't mean writing a good book or being a great cop. Or in Henry's case, being an actor. What do you think you can do to help others?" He thought about it and said he didn't know. "Yes you do. You're afraid of failing at it. I can see the idea right there in your head."

"I wish that others like us could speak up for themselves." Quincey asked him how he'd do that. "By being gay and not hiding behind it any longer."

"That's the ticket." Quincey stood up and put out his hand. Paddy took it into his and felt something powerful run down his arm. "You're going to be good at that as well."

"Wait. What?" But he was gone.

Chapter 13

Henry signed the contract, and was still reeling from the amount of money he was going to get from this movie. He'd never made much more than scale since he'd been in the business. And he was going to get a percentage of the ticket price for as long as it was in theatres, as well as movie rental rights. He looked over at Jake when he laughed.

"I should have had you a long time ago as my attorney." Jake laughed harder. "Christ, you're a real hard ass when you want to be, aren't you?"

"Yes. Especially for my friends. Are you happy with all of this? Not just the money, Henry, but everything." He told him he was. "Good. I think that having it in your contacts from now on about being able to have Paddy nearby is a good thing for you. No scandals to chase you later."

That had been a complete surprise when Jake had said that was what he wanted. Having Paddy not just nearby, but able to share his trailer with him and on set all the time was going to be relaxing as well. There were other perks too. Some of them were small—Jake said that they were in there to be tossed out when they were negotiating—but bigger things too. Like his pay.

He was going to be a headliner in this epic movie. Not only that, but they were also to consult him before there were any changes to his character, and he got to select his own clothing. It was like Jake said…they had asked for him, he'd not gone looking.

"This will make you a hotter item as well. With you making so much, movie companies will figure that if this company thought you were worth it, then they'll want you too. But you have to do what I told you or this could all go belly up for you." He was to not get into trouble, not that he ever did, and be as cooperative as he could without being a pushover. "You're going to be a household name, Henry. I'm so happy for you."

"When people find out that you did this for me, you're going to have other actors beating a path to your door." Jake only winked at him. "You sly devil you. How about that."

They were both still laughing when they headed out of the offices.

There was a group of people outside the building. There was usually a crowd like this when he had come to the offices here. They were waiting for a big name to come out, and they wanted an autograph or picture with whoever it was. Henry nearly walked by them when one of them asked if he was Henry Myers, the actor.

"I am. Is there something I can help you with?" Jake laughed, and the man gushed. Like he was seeing his hero or something. When he asked for his autograph, he signed a picture of himself that he'd had taken a few months before the end of the last movie he'd been in. Then he did the same with the rest of the people there...signing pictures or taking selfie pictures with them.

"I think you liked that." Jake and he were in the limo that had brought them to the office. The two of them were staying in the same hotel, but not the same room. He said they had to give the look of being only lawyer to client, and not good friends. "You sure made their day. Get used to that, Henry, from now on. If you play your cards right, you'll be getting that much more. And the men you just spoke to will come to you rather than the other way around."

He could get used to this. And when he pulled out his cell phone to call Paddy, he was nearly too excited to press the right buttons. Paddy asked him how it went, and all Henry could talk about was the crowd outside waiting for him.

"You're a big star and they know it. Christ, I wish that I could have been there. This is so great." He said that he wished he could have too. "You and I will have dinner out as soon as I see you."

"I'd love that. All of us. Jake said that I'm going to be big now." Paddy told him that he was now. "I just can't believe this. It's like a dream come true for me. I really wish you were here."

"Look up." He was confused for a second as they were let out of the limo. "To your right, dork."

And there he was. Paddy and the rest of them were standing right outside the restaurant where he and Jake were going to have dinner. Christy had a large bouquet of flowers, and as soon as he took them from her, Paddy told him they were from him. It was the best kind of gift that he could have been given. His family there with him to celebrate. Even Jenna was with them, and Henry kissed her as well.

The restaurant was packed, but they were shown to a table right away. The studio had called ahead, they were told, and said to treat him and his family well. They were even picking up the tab on this, and Henry was almost embarrassed. But Jake told him again to get used to it.

Pictures were taken of them all together, and he and Paddy had some of just the two of them. Things were going really fast for them, and he didn't want to miss a single thing about it. He asked Jake how he'd planned this.

"It was easy. You were so nervous that I could have told you that a bomb was under your bed and you would have nodded and said how terrified you were." Henry said that he was a little. "A little? That's an understatement if I've ever heard one."

The dinner was delicious. And the people around him made it so much better. Everyone ordered something different, and they had fun sharing what they had gotten. And when the dessert cart came to them, all those beautiful and fattening things on it, he nearly turned it away when Christy asked if they could have it all. When Jake nodded, it was like having his cake and having lots of whipped cream on it as well.

"You do know that you will burn more calories than before as my mate." He felt his face heat up when Paddy spoke. "Not with sex, though that does help. No, with my wolf, and every time I nip at you, you take a little more of me into you. Denny told me that we should see all kinds of changes in you over the next few months. You might not be able to shift, but you'll take on all the characteristics of a wolf."

"So it is sex." Christy smiled at him when he winked. "I might be a dummy, but I know what sex is. And while I can see Paddy getting ready to tell me I'm not a dummy, I am on some things. But smarter than he is on other stuff."

"All right, I'll give you that. But you're my sister, and if anyone calls you that other than you, then you only have to tell me. I'll make sure they pay." Christy promised Henry that she would. And loved that he thought of her as his sister too. "I do, love. You are the best thing that's happened to Paddy and me."

They decided to head home. The plane was on the tarmac and ready for them anyway. Henry wanted to be in his own bed in his home. Celebrating was a blast, but he had to get back to the real world now. And he had lines to learn. His part in this thing was bigger than he'd had before, and he didn't want to flub it up. Besides, he wanted to be with Paddy tonight.

They landed at just before midnight their time. Everyone was exhausted, and Henry was glad that there was something there to pick them up. As they were headed home, he thought of the upcoming holidays and all the things he was going to be able to do. First and foremost, he was going to play in the snow, something that he'd never done before.

Henry had only been gone two days, but the difference that the house had taken on was amazing. Paddy's things had arrived from Cincinnati and were stored in the barn. The few things that he really wanted were already placed in his office.

Paddy had his computer set up, as well as a printer and a large desk. He had wanted to start out slow, but his excitement had grown so much over this that Jake and Forrest had talked him into getting what he needed now and not to skimp.

In addition to the office that Paddy was using, they had staff too. Sarah was their cook, and would be forever if she wanted. There were maids to help with the everyday upkeep on the house. Someone had been hired to take care of the lawn and trees, and there had been a crew of people working in the cemetery.

It had been a jumbled mess back there. An iron fence had been put around the large area, but it had long since fallen to disrepair, as well as vines and weeds had pulled it over in other places. The headstones were in good shape, and Henry thought it was because no one had found the place, so they'd never been vandalized.

Henry got up early the next morning and made his way back there. Paddy was still asleep, and Christy was off to work. Walking in the deep woods, it was just chilly enough for a jacket.

He could see the cemetery was taking shape even before he got to it. Seventeen headstones were upright, and a half dozen or so were flush with the ground. He was saddened by the dates on most of them, the children that had only been days old when they passed, and even some of the children hadn't made it to ten years of age when they died.

There hadn't been a headstone for Howie when they'd first come here. But he had one now, its shape and stone much like the others that were there. He sat on the bench nearby, the one that Grant said that his father had placed there for their mother when she visited. Looking at the deer playing nearby, he was startled when a woman came to see him.

"You're stronger than the other gentleman that comes here. I didn't think I'd get to thank anyone for bringing my boys both home to me." He looked to where she was standing; the mother of the twins had died when she was only in her thirties. "I've been haunting here for a long time now."

194

"I'm sorry for your loss, Mrs. Sheppard." She nodded and looked at the markers with their names on them. "You have wonderful sons. I've talked to them both, and have enjoyed their company."

"Howie talks to me now too. And I've talked to Grant. He's a good boy too. I hated that they went away so young, but there was war and they wished to do their part. I missed them every day." He said he was sorry again. "I should have had more children. But having them boys nearly took me out. My husband said he'd not put me through that again and refused to talk about it. I loved him. A lot of women that I know only tolerated their husbands, but Hamilton, he was good to us. And he loved me too."

"Of course he did." She smiled and sat down on her headstone. "It's nice that you can be here with them after so long, don't you think?"

"I'm not long for this world, young man. But I do have something for you to give to the other gentleman, the one writing the book for my boys. You tell him that at the end of the old barn, way on back there, there is a grave like none of the others. I don't remember the name that was put on it, but it's different. You tell him to go and get it." Henry told her that he couldn't take it to a relative. "I know that. I do. But it's for him. When the war started, and my boys were set on going, Hamilton and I, we put all our things in a big old can. It was metal, hard to come by back then. But he worked at sealing it up good so that nothing would get to it. The darkies that are back there, they weren't none of them ours. We didn't sit well with how they was treated, and we just let them come and have a meal with us like they was regular people. Because that's what they were. Just people with a different colored skin."

"Thank you for that. We still have a few issues with that even today." She nodded as if she knew that too. "What's in this can, if you don't mind me asking? I don't want him hurt."

"He told me that you two were in love. I don't know how that's to work, but he seemed happy and that's all that matters. But that can, it holds all the things we found dear to our hearts. And some money. Not much, but there are some pictures too of the homestead we had. It cost a pretty penny, that did, to have done. Why, for about thirty cents we could have had our likeness put on a stamp to use. What do you think of that?" She laughed. "You go on and dig it up for him and you. And if you've a mind to, you could make it pretty back there for them too. I used to, but...well, I can't no more."

"We'll do that. I'll get a start on it as soon as we find it. I don't know that the barn is still there, to be honest." She told him that the foundation was there, but the wood was about all gone now. "I'll look for it today."

When she left him there, telling him that she had said her goodbyes to her boys, Henry sat there for several minutes. Paddy joined him a few minutes later, and they walked to the barn. He was as excited for this new adventure as he was the movie. Henry couldn't wait to find what treasures were in the can.

~~~

Cameron kept his head down as he walked to the store. There were too many people out for him to make it without someone touching him, and today, he just wasn't in the mood to deal with people and their issues. Keeping his hands in his pockets helped, but there were people that were never aware of their surroundings and they would touch him.

"Hello, Mr. Henderson." He nodded at the store manager as he walked by him. One of the few people that he knew that seemed to have a good grip on keeping out of his way. "We're having a sale on ham today. I was hoping I could convince you to partake."

Something was wrong. Not just with the man, but the store as well. He didn't bother looking around, but put his hand out to the man, thanking him for letting him know about the sale that Cameron couldn't care less about. As soon as he touched him, Cameron saw the pain come over the manager's face.

He'd take care of him later, but for now, there was trouble. The store was being robbed, and he'd walked in on it inadvertently. Cameron reached out for his sister, Caitlynn, to tell her what was going on.

I know. I nearly shit myself when you walked in the place. Don't you ever turn on the television or listen to the radio? Fuck Cam, you're right in the middle of a hostage situation. He told her that she knew why he didn't, and walked back to where the ham was. He figured that was where things were going down. *What do you see? Since you're there, you might as well help us.*

His sister was a cop. A good one too. And he was sure that part of her being a good cop was because he could help her. Not all the time, but enough that she closed more cases than most did, and people liked her. While few people even wanted to be in the same room with him.

I'm thinking of buying a ham. According to Mr. Sharp, they're on sale today. He wants me to partake. He looked at the hams in the bin. *How does one buy a ham, Cattie my dear?*

I haven't the foggiest idea. Usually, if I have a craving for some, I tell cook. What the hell are you seeing, Cam? Besides hams. He laughed and reached out to see what was there. *Don't get hurt. Mom will have a conniption if you do.*

There are seven men behind the glass in the meat department. They have six people with them. Each of them have been roughed up, but not killed. Mr. Sharp is up front with two of the men. Plus one is sitting in front of the vault with a gun pointed at him until I leave. Very inhospitable, don't you think? All she said was his name. *There are two more bad guys around back. If you go there now, they're both having a smoke...pot, I do believe, which has them slightly distracted. They're the getaway cars.*

Why the store? I mean, there is a bank right around the corner. He said he'd check. *Cam, I'm not sure if I tell you enough, but I love you.* He paused in what he was doing to think about what she'd just said to him.

Why are you telling me that now? Are you in trouble? She said she wasn't, but he was helping her. *Don't scare me like that again. I need you.*

And I need you. In two minutes the ones around back will be taken care of. He put a ham, the biggest one he could find, into his little cart and moved to the vegetables. *What are you doing now?*

I needed some salad fixings. That's why I risked coming here to get. If I get out of here alive, I'm going to have a nice salad. She told him she'd buy him one when he got out of there. *No need, my dear. I know what you make as a cop.*

Cam, we have more money than the banks around here. I can afford to buy my little brother a salad when I want to. She was pissy. Cattie got that way when she was stressed. *Okay, two down. Where are you now? Still looking at lettuce?*

No, I've decided that if you're going to buy me a salad, I need nothing else. Cattie, are you coming in the back way? She said that she wasn't, but the others were. *All right. If you come in the front when I tell you, I'll have the those men taken care of. I promise you, I won't be hurt.*

He moved up to the cash register and Mr. Sharp came out of the office to ring him out. Cam was carrying, and knew how to use his gun better than his sister. He'd had more practice at killing too.

Cam pulled his ham out of his cart, and instead of putting it on the conveyer belt, he shoved it at Mr. Sharp, taking him to the floor. When the other men popped their heads up to see what had happened, Cam shot both of them in the head. Waiting on number three, he told Cattie to come in and join them. As soon as the door swished open, he shot the third man as he sprinted to the back.

Before You Go...

HELP AN AUTHOR

write a review

THANK YOU!

Share your voice and help guide other readers to these wonderful books. Even if it's only a line or two your reviews help readers discover the author's books so they can continue creating stories that you'll love. Login to your favorite retailer and leave a review. Thank you.

Kathi Barton, winner of the Pinnacle Book Achievement award as well as a best-selling author on Amazon and All Romance books, lives in Nashport, Ohio with her husband Paul. When not creating new worlds and romance, Kathi and her husband enjoy camping and going to auctions. She can also be seen at county fairs with her husband who is an artist and potter.

Her muse, a cross between Jimmy Stewart and Hugh Jackman, brings her stories to life for her readers in a way that has them coming back time and again for more. Her favorite genre is paranormal romance with a great deal of spice. You can visit Kathi online and drop her an email if you'd like. She loves hearing from her fans. aaronskiss@gmail.com.

Follow Kathi on her blog: http://kathisbartonauthor. blogspot.com/

www.ingramcontent.com/pod-product-compliance
Lightning Source LLC
Chambersburg PA
CBHW032001170626
46807CB00006B/2585